ANGEL MAGIC

Book 2

The Mage's Daughter Trilogy

S.A. BECK

This is a work of fiction. Names, characters, organizations,places, events, and incidents are either products of the author's imagination or are used fictitiously.

ISBN: 978-1-987859-40-9

CONTENTS

CHAPTER 1
Life Without Mercy

Ines knew before she rounded the corner that she had found a demon. The sounds of its influence were clear—two human voices raised in an argument so fierce and irrational that it filled the surrounding fields.

Crouching behind the hedgerow, Ines made the most of her small size to stay hidden while she caught a glimpse of what was happening. Tightening her grip on a long kitchen knife, its blade sharpened to a deadly edge, she watched the argument. One man looked as if he belonged in the countryside, with his cloth cap and his mud-stained pants. The other was completely out of place in a brand-name tracksuit far, far cleaner and less battered than Ines's practical jogging bottoms and hoodie. His baseball cap bore an Arsenal logo that would have quadrupled its price.

As the argument rose and the track-suited man shoved the farmer, a dark figure stood in the road behind them, rubbing its tentacle-like fingers against each other in glee. Hundreds of eyes peered excitedly from between the sharp spines that covered the rest of its head. The chemosh demon looked almost giddy with excitement.

It would have been unsettling to see such a human response in that gray, menacing Hell beast if not for the other demons Ines had met.

This wasn't one to negotiate with and certainly not to befriend. Unseen by the arguing humans, it reached out and stroked the sides of their faces, feeding off their fury even as it amplified it. Spittle flew with the city dweller's rage-filled words. The farmer lifted a spade from the bank behind him, pulling it back, ready to strike.

It was now or never.

Ines dashed from her hiding place, trainers pounding the dozen yards between her and the demon. Flinging herself through the gap between the startled humans, she leapt straight at the abomination, knife raised, thrusting with all her might.

The blade sank into the chemosh's chest. Black, sticky blood sprayed out, coating Ines and spattering the others. The chemosh flailed wildly with one arm, while with the other it grabbed hold of Ines. Tentacles tangled with her ponytail, dragging her toward the spikes on its face. She pulled back the knife and stabbed again and again. Flesh writhed beneath her blows as the chemosh shifted its flesh, trying to repair the wounded spot.

But she was ready. She attacked over and over, venting all her pain and frustration in wild fury. Her anger at the demons, her agony at the absence of her parents, the horrifying experiences that woke her sweating in the night—all of it went into those blows, hacking the chemosh apart as it tried to recover.

Spines pressed against her cheek as the demon drew her closer. Its other arm had withered almost to nothing, its mass gone to protecting the damaged chest. The demon drew flesh from its legs, keeping one arm strong to fight Ines. As its legs grew thinner, its mass top heavy, it started to wobble.

The spines were pressing into Ines's face now. Her own blood dribbled hot down her cheek. Yet she barely felt the pain, too caught up in the moment, driven by adrenaline and her newfound ferocity.

Unable to balance, the chemosh fell back onto the road. Ines went with it, using the force of the fall to drive the knife deeper into the demon's chest. As they hit the ground, she let go of the handle and rolled clear, arm outstretched in a breakfall. Rolling through the movement, she sprang straight back to her feet. Spinning around, she kicked the knife handle. The blade spun free, ripping a deep hole in the chest of the writhing demon. There was a final spurt of blood, and it lay still.

Ines took a deep breath. She was trembling from head to toe, caught in the aftermath of the adrenaline rush and in the relief of still being alive. Not exactly delight, but a satisfaction that only these moments could bring.

The two men stared in horror at the body of the demon. The human mind might be trained not to see the creatures of Heaven and Hell, but there came a point when they became impossible to ignore.

"You're welcome." Ines picked up the knife, wiped the blood from it on a handful of grass, and stuck it back into the improvised sheath at her waist.

The farmer looked at her, looked down at the black demonic blood with which he was spattered, screamed, and ran.

"You look well messed up." The other man was clearly fighting his fear, trying to focus on concern for Ines. "You're a bit young to be wandering around with a knife."

"I'm sixteen." Ines glared at him. "I'm legally old enough to have sex or drop out of school. I can cope with this better than you can."

She turned and jogged off down the road, back toward Barnet and home.

* * *

She tried to come back into the house quietly, so as not to upset Toby. London was peaceful since she had brought down the Ministry of Occult Affairs's schemes. No angels or demons openly toying with people's emotions. None of the riots and random crime that had blighted the city a few weeks ago. Even out here in the suburbs, it was a safe place to be—as safe as anywhere in Britain right now. She didn't want to remind her kid brother of the dangers waiting half a mile down the road.

But the problem with twelve-year-olds was that they could be surprisingly observant. Or just in the wrong place at the wrong time.

Toby stared at her through the doorway of the living room. He had a pile of brightly colored magazines scattered around him, where he'd been flicking between pictures of wrestlers and stories about giant robots fighting each other. He had been reverting over the past few weeks, descending deeper into the things he had loved a year or two before, hiding from the horrible present for hours at a time, only to emerge and take a chilling interest in it.

"You're covered in blood." He tilted his head to one side, his hair flopping in an unruly manner around his head. "Some of it's yours."

"Only a little," Ines said. "Don't worry about it."

"I watched the news." Toby flung aside his magazine. Biscuit crumbs fell from his T-shirt and jeans as he stood up. "There's more trouble. They talked about fires in Bristol and riots in Norwich. Didn't we go to Norwich once?"

"A holiday on the broads." Ines walked into the living room. She'd given up on not getting stains on the carpet. Between her kills and Toby's comfort eating, that was one battle she couldn't win. "We went into Norwich one day and met up with…"

The words trailed off. Elizabeth Oldfield had been her mother's closest friend. Her betrayal, and her part in weakening the Barrier of Mercy, made Ines feel as if she'd been punched in the gut. For all she knew, Elizabeth still had their parents captive and was still working on bringing down the Barrier, drawing on its power for whatever schemes she and the Ministry of Occult Affairs had for the world.

Forcing a smile, Ines ruffled Toby's hair with her cleaner hand, the one that hadn't held the knife.

"It'll be okay, kiddo," she said.

"Don't call me kiddo." Toby squirmed away from her and folded his arms across his chest. "You're not Mum or Dad. You don't get to talk to me like that."

"Oh, don't I?" Anger flared inside her. "Who's been cooking your meals? Who's been washing your clothes? Who's been protecting you from all the awful things out there?"

"Damon." Now Toby sounded angry. "You wouldn't even have cooked last night if he hadn't been here. And I don't need my clothes washed. They're fine as they are."

"No, they aren't." Ines took a deep breath. She could smell her brother even through the demon stench and her own sweat. "When was the last time you took a shower?"

"I'm never having a shower," Toby shouted. "And I'm never doing what you say!"

He ran past her, up the stairs, and slammed his bedroom door behind him.

Ines sighed. She didn't have the energy for this. She knew that she should, that Toby needed her no matter what he said. He was too young to look after himself. Maybe they both were, but one of them had to do it, and she was the oldest. But every evening she looked at him, whether he sat hollow eyed in front of the TV or curled up by her side, clutching her close and crying for their parents, and she knew that she felt the same way. It was as if a deep pit had opened up inside her, and she wanted to fall into it. To let go and descend into oblivion. To weep and wail until there was nothing left to cry over, no feelings left. Only then, if there was anything left of her, might she emerge on the other side.

But she couldn't let go. Not when Toby needed her to look after him. Not when their parents needed her to find them, to rescue them from wherever they were held. No one else was going to do these things.

Trudging down the corridor and into the kitchen, she pondered what to do now. She needed a shower and a change of clothes. At least then she wouldn't be wearing sticky reminders of the fight.

First, though, she needed a drink and food to fill her growling belly.

On the kitchen counter was a large glass of water and a plate piled high with cheese-and-pickle sandwiches. Next to them was a note:

"I thought you'd be idiot enough to go out fighting before breakfast. This is to stop you biting Toby's head off in your hunger. Gone to talk with a dog about a man. Back soon. D."

A smile spread across Ines's face as warmth and hope emerged from the depths of her weary heart. Sometimes it seemed as if Damon knew her better than she did.

Aware of what a mess she looked, she tucked loose strands of hair back into her ponytail then reached for a sandwich. It was just ordinary bread and cheap cheese—what they could afford without her parents around to do the shopping. But there was a layer of homemade chutney in there, from her dad's pickling phase the previous summer. Carrot-and-cauliflower chutney was one of the worst things he'd made, but the taste of it—sweet and tangy and slightly burned—made her smile even more.

Gobbling down a second sandwich, she picked up the plate and headed up the stairs. She stopped outside Toby's room and knocked gently on the door. Someone was looking after her—the least she could do was share that thoughtfulness.

"Damon left us Dad sandwiches," she said gently. There was no reply. "I'll just leave them here."

She placed the plate on the floor and carried on down the landing, set on a hot shower.

Behind her, Toby's bedroom door opened. Like a birdwatcher near her goal, she didn't dare turn around for fear of spooking the little creature she had drawn out of its nest. Instead, she slowed her pace.

"Thank you." Toby's voice was quiet, a small thing almost lost in the silence of their world. He sounded as though he'd been crying. "I'm sorry. You're not Mum or Dad, but some days you're the best."

The door closed again.

Something terrible and tense finally broke inside Ines. Tears ran down her face as she stepped into the bathroom. Closing the door behind her, safe and alone in the white, clean space, she slid to the floor and let herself cry.

CHAPTER 2
Family

Walking into the study made Ines feel safe, in a way that the rest of the house didn't. Her home had been violated by a demon attack. She had fought to the death against her first chemosh in the kitchen. Though home was still home, she always felt a little on edge. The house was a family space, belonging to a family who were half missing. It was a space she was meant to share with them, and their absence was unsettling. And, so, by a paradox of emotion, the study had become her safe place.

She had seldom been allowed in here growing up. It was her parents' working space. They had not wanted to be interrupted, as much for the sake of their children as for that of their work. Magic could be a dangerous business, and Toby's fledgling gift for it hadn't made it any safer. So the room was kept locked, against her, against her brother, and against a world that, she now understood, included all manner of threats to a mage: angels, demons, even battles with their own colleagues and competitors. This was the world for which her parents had prepared her, even as they sheltered her from magic itself.

The disconnection between her life and what went on in the room made it feel even more like her parents' space. A safe place into which ordinary matters didn't intrude. Her only memories of being there as a kid had involved being held safely in her mother's lap or prodding at the piles of old computers around her father's desk. She felt her parents' presence more here than in any other part of the house.

In their absence, Ines had let the chaos of her dad's side of the room spread. Piles of papers littered the carpet in front of the barred windows. Heaps of files teetered on boxes she had pulled them out of. The filing cabinet hung permanently open. Even some of those old computers hummed away, ready for Ines to dive in and have another try at understanding her dad's esoteric filing systems.

None of it had done her any good. After weeks of delving through these files, she was still no closer to knowing where the Ministry of Occult Affairs might have taken her parents. Many places were referred to in the files: testing grounds, office buildings, research labs, and arcane sites scattered up and down the country. Some staffed by the Ministry, some casually watched, others largely ignored as far as she could tell from the way they were described. But none was listed as a prison, jail, or safe house. The study might be comforting, but the piles of paper weren't.

A soft tapping on the study door drew her attention. She looked up from where she sat, cross-legged among a sprawl of old paperwork, to see Damon smiling across the room.

"That's quite a nest you've built for yourself there." He leaned against the doorframe, a tall, slim figure dressed in black from head to toe, his skin pale. "Are you sure you're not some kind of bird? I hear that owls are smart, if not terribly sociable."

"Like you were ever sociable." Ines jumped to her feet and crossed the room to hug him. "Thank you for my sandwiches. You were right. I got carried away and forgot about eating."

"I'm always right." Damon hugged her in return, an awkward embrace but one she enjoyed. "It's the burden of genius."

"Or just the burden of demonhood?" Ines grinned. "I've heard that Lucifer could be pretty arrogant."

"Not funny." Damon frowned and took a step back.

"Sorry." Ines shifted uncomfortably from foot to foot. "I just..."

"It's not you." Damon sighed. "I am who I am, and sooner or later, I'm going to have to accept that even being half demon isn't off limits. Still, not my favorite topic of conversation." He reached into the satchel hanging at his waist and pulled out a notebook. "That said, it has its uses. Do you want to hear the latest?"

"Of course!"

Before Ines could go any further, there was a sound of feet pounding down the stairs. Ines pushed Damon out of the study and into the living room, closing the door behind her. This might be her place of comfort, but she still wanted to keep Toby safe from the secrets that lay inside, and the powers they connected to.

"Damon!" Toby rushed into the room, ran halfway to the older boy, and then seemed to remember that he was a cool, calm twelve-year-old. He stopped in the middle of the room, stuck his hands in his pockets, and tried to look casual. "What's up, man?"

A smile struggled to break free from Damon's face, a cute little expression that made Ines want to reach out and touch his cheek. After a flickering moment, it disappeared, replaced by the same seriousness with which Toby was looking at him.

"Hey, Toby." Damon reached back into his bag. "I got you something."

He pulled out a handful of magazines and handed them over.

"Cool!" Forgetting his attempt to play it cool, Toby snatched the magazines and flung himself down on the sofa, spreading them out to pick the best one. "Where did you get them?"

"The big newsagents have their supply chains up and running again." Damon shrugged. "My mum picked these up after I talked about what you enjoy doing."

"Brilliant." Toby flicked through the magazines for half a minute before remembering his manners. "Thanks, Damon. And say thank you to your mum for me."

The sound of rustling paper filled the room while Damon smiled fondly at the younger boy. This was one more thing about him that amazed Ines. There were times when she could barely stand her kid brother, but Damon had formed an instant bond with him. They chatted in a way that she struggled to do with either of them, and that made her jealous. After all, Damon was her friend. They had always been relaxed and comfortable around each other. But something had changed in the past month.

"We're going to make a cuppa." Taking Damon's arm, she led him into the kitchen and shut the door behind them. As she filled the kettle, she started on the serious side of the conversation. "What have you found out?"

Damon grabbed mugs from the cupboard and dropped teabags into them. He'd been around so much recently, sleeping on the sofa every other night, he was as familiar with the house as Ines was.

"The Barrier of Mercy is still crumbling." He looked at Ines and then away. "What you did at Oldfield's estate stopped the Ministry draining power from it, but the damage has been done. The Barrier is crumbling, and it's starting to affect the rest of the country."

"So why are things going back to normal?" Ines asked. "Why aren't we seeing demons and angels around London?"

"I talked with some of my father's smarter minions. They think that it's a reaction to what happened to London before. So much strain was put on the Barrier here, when you took off that strain by stopping Oldfield, the Barrier over the city rushed back into place, becoming stronger than ever. Like a rubber band flying back into shape when you let go."

"That doesn't make any sense." The tea made, Ines took a sip of hers. "Rubber bands aren't like walls or magic spells."

"Nothing is quite like magic spells." Damon shrugged.

They sat and drank in silence for a few moments. Damon looked exhausted. Of the two of them, he was the only one with contacts in the magical world, so he'd been the one going out to gather news, as well as keeping an eye on his mum over in Islington. Yet here he was, coming back to her again and again.

As he stared down at his mug, a glazed look in his eyes, Ines watched her friend. The change that had come between them wasn't all bad. There might not be the relaxed laughter of more peaceful times, but she felt closer to him than ever. It would have been impossible for things to remain the same, but now she was caught trying to understand where they were going.

The Damon she now knew was something of a hero. He had saved her several times, both with his magic and by talking people around. There was strength in him she had never seen before, that had carried him through in defiance of his father, the demon lord Chron. This wasn't just one more teenager like her, but someone who could face the most terrifying entities in the world. The half-demon part had alarmed her at first, but there was an allure to that as well, a bad-boy charm that was hard to resist.

She looked away, unsettled by the hammering of her heart. Damon was her best friend. She might have wanted something more once, but surely not now? Not when they were in danger like this. Not when she had been kissed by an angel.

At the thought of Rumiel, her heart beat even faster. Her cup shook in her hands at the memory of yet another betrayal.

"Are you all right?" Damon reached out and laid his hand on hers. It was warmer than he looked, the touch gentler than she expected.

"I'm fine." She set the mug aside and took his hand, looking at him across the breakfast counter. "I'm just frustrated. I'm getting nowhere tracking down Mum and Dad. The information you've brought helps us understand what's happening, but none of it is about them."

She hesitated, not knowing whether to cross this next line, and it was as if

Damon looked into her very soul, seeing the thing she had been about to ask. He drew his hand back and shook his head.

"I won't do it," he said. "Not unless things get really desperate. This power I have, it's not a good power. It comes from pain and misery. Whatever I achieve by using my magic, someone suffers along the way. And trying to track your parents down, that would take a lot of suffering."

"I'm already in pain." Ines was surprised at the sharpness of her tone, then angry with herself for being caught unawares, and angry with Damon for not understanding. "I'm already suffering. Let me fuel the magic. I can take more pain if that's what it needs. I'll take whatever's needed to find my parents."

"It's not that simple." Damon stood and turned away from her. He started rummaging through the cupboard, as if there were anything there he might want, as if he didn't already know exactly where everything was. "My power is limited. I can do things with time—freeze it in a small area, reach through it for information if I'm lucky. But it's not exact—it won't always do what you want."

"What do we lose by trying?"

"Me." Damon turned to face her, his expression grim. He stared into her eyes. "Every time I give in to that power, every time I let the demon out, I risk losing a part of who I am. I become someone who is powered by horror and misery. If I keep doing that, I might start enjoying it. That's what power does. It makes people want more. And I don't want to be someone who craves the misery of others.

"I'll do anything for you, Ines, whatever the cost to me, if I think it'll work. But I won't destroy others for a million-to-one shot, not until we're out of other options."

He put his mug in the sink and walked slowly toward the door.

"Damon..." Ines felt as if she were frozen, her body and mind unwilling to obey her. She didn't even know what she wanted to say. Did she want to beg him to help her or to forgive her? Did she want to hug him or plead with him? The one thing she knew for certain was that she didn't want to lose him.

"Ask me anything else," Damon said quietly as he left the room. "But not that."

CHAPTER 3
Why Mages Live in Hackney

"Of course there are mages in Hackney." Damon raised an eyebrow. "They get everywhere, and especially the places that are gentrifying. Sure, they like a good source of power or a place with plenty of dusty libraries. But what most mages love, what really gets them going in the morning, is cheap housing and trendy coffee bars."

"Really?" Ines thought of her parents. They had never been trendy as far as she was aware. But then her dad did love good coffee, and house prices were among her mum's few non-magical interests.

"Of course not." Damon smiled and shook his head. "You think everyone who uses magic is some kind of middle-class hipster?" He looked up thoughtfully at the ceiling of the Tube carriage. "Though that begs the question, is there any other sort of hipster?"

"What's he on about?" Toby peered around Ines at their friend, a puzzled expression on his face.

"He thinks he's being funny." Ines pulled a chocolate bar from her pocket. "Here."

She felt sadness in watching her brother gobble down the chocolate. Sweets were a good distraction and practically the only way she had of getting him to do what she wanted. But he was turning more and more to food as a source of comfort. In the short time they'd been without their parents, he'd already started to put on weight. She worried about what it was doing to him. Being heavy and slow would have driven her mad as well as made her vulnerable to all the dangers she'd met. Then there was diabetes—she didn't know much about it, but she had a vague idea that sweet foods led to it, and that it could kill you when you got older.

What she was doing might hurt her brother in the long term, but in the short term, it was hard to resist seeing him happy, if only for as long as it took to wolf down a snack and lick his fingers clean.

"You didn't have to bring me." Toby looked up at her, responding to her concerned expression with a defiant one of his own. "I can look after myself, you know."

"Can you fight off mages?" Ines asked. "Or demons, or angels?"

"I know some magic." Toby held the empty chocolate wrapper out in his open palm. The fingers of his other hand danced in the air, and the wrapper moved in response, turning into the shape of one of his robot toys.

Ines snatched it from his hand, glancing around the car to see if anyone was watching. A drunk with a wild beard, tobacco-stained fingers, and a woolly hat gazed at them groggily, shook his head, and went back to sleep. Nobody else was watching, or if they were, then they lived by the code of the Tube: don't talk, don't make eye contact, don't treat each other like human beings. Apparently, that was what adults did to stay sane in the packed confines of London's streets and transport system.

Sometimes Ines longed to reach full adulthood, with all the benefits it could bring. But, other times, she was glad she hadn't gained such a jaded view of the world.

The darkness outside the window turned to bright light as they emerged from a tunnel into the cold, pale expanse of a tube station. As the doors hissed open, Ines led the boys out onto the platform and from there swiftly up the stairs and out through the ticket barriers, into a sunny, bustling street.

"Which way?" She turned to Damon, who was turning his gold pocket watch between his thin fingers.

"This way." He led them down the road, sliding between other pedestrians, down a side street and into a narrow alley, each turn taking them farther from human activity. An old woman in a bright-blue headscarf passed them with a shopping bag, blinking as if in surprise at the sight of three young people treading the same streets as her.

A minute later, they emerged into a wide space between 1960s housing blocks. In one way, it was completely ordinary, the sort of concrete space incorporated into many ill-planned housing projects. Its gray slabs were unappealing to play on, its flower beds neglected, its benches covered with decades of graffiti.

In another way, it was completely unique.

Ines had been to plenty of markets, but never one quite like this. The stalls that filled the courtyard looked as if they had been plucked from a hundred different countries and every era in history, jumbled together and dropped down in the middle of London. The stall-holders mostly wore modern clothes, and ordinary ones at that, looking like the men and women who ran fruit and veg stalls up and down the country. But the structures they served from, and the wares piled up inside them, were beyond belief.

Damon led them past an open-front teepee, in which strange creatures hung, tied to hooks as if in a butcher's window. They looked as if they had been skinned, until one reared its long pink neck and gnashed at the air behind the stallholder.

Next was a stall with a sign that read Alchemical Extracts. Jars and bottles glowed on its shelves, the liquids inside them swirling and glittering. One was only half full, and the liquid inside it spun like a whirlwind.

There were magical florists, suppliers of ingredients for spells, and a second-hand bookstall whose stock was covered in all manner of strange leathers and stranger scripts.

"Is this a mages' market?" Ines asked in surprise.

"What else?" Damon grinned.

"But how... Why... Wouldn't other people..."

"It's like angels and demons," he said. "You have to be looking to see it."

They stopped at the bookstall. A man sat in a deck chair to one side, his battered top hat out of place when worn with jeans and an Adidas top. He tipped the hat to them in greeting then glanced past them, eyeing the other shoppers with the look of a man who had learned to beware the world and its surprises.

"Damon." The stallholder pushed himself out of his seat. "You got my message."

"I did, Frank." Damon held out a paper bag. "Here, one favor for another."

Frank opened the bag and smiled.

"American jelly beans." He took one and held it up, examining it like a precious gem in the light. "So fake. So inhuman. So incredibly tasty. You know my curse stops me shopping in the places they stock these?"

He closed his eyes and popped the sweet into his mouth. A look of delight filled his face.

"I know." Damon caught Ines's eye and shook his head. "That's why I brought them."

Frank's eyes shot open.

"No need to patronize me, young man." He put the jelly beans in one pocket and pulled a piece of paper out of the other. "Especially not when I've got this for you."

"Really?" Damon took the sheet of paper and frowned at its contents. "This is where the Salgados are being kept?"

"Ssh!" Frank grabbed Damon's arm and ushered them around the side of the stall, out of sight of the rest of the market. "There've been some other folks making inquiries since you were here last. Don't think you want to draw attention to yourselves, saying things like that."

"What's wrong with saying my name?" Ines clenched her fists, ready for trouble in whatever form it came.

"So you're David and Julie's kid?" Frank glanced at Toby. "Both of you are?"

"Where's my mum?" Toby glared daggers at the bookseller, but his voice sounded small and frightened.

"Sorry, son, I don't know that." Frank pulled the jelly beans out of his pocket and held the bag out to Toby. "Just one, mind. A peace offering." He watched with eagle eyes as Toby picked out a green jelly bean. "That on the paper isn't where your folks are at, but it should—"

A bright flash filled air, leaving spots across Ines's vision. A commotion rose from the far side of the stall—people yelling, others running, the thump of things being knocked to the ground.

Ines didn't wait to see how anyone else responded. Her hand went straight up her sleeve, drawing one of the knives she kept there. She ran around the stall.

Three figures hung in the air above the market, golden wings flapping at their backs. In the center stood the Archangel Michael, leader of the Blazing Host. Long white hair flew with the wind from his beating wings, and the flames on his sword flickered with a light almost as bright as the sun. To his left was Sanctus, with his boxer's body and his loose white tracksuit, brass knuckles glowing white.

But though their presence was intimidating, it was the third angel who made Ines's breath catch in her throat.

Rumiel was as handsome as the first day she had seen him. Blond, tanned, with the face of a model and a smile that made her heart glow, even as the memory of his treachery gouged at her mind. His hands were held wide as if in welcome.

"Ines." His voice filled the air. "At last, we have found you. I had all but given up hope."

"How the hell did you get here?" Ines focused on her anger instead of her desire. "London is meant to be safe."

"Nothing can stand against the Host," Michael roared. As he did so, Ines realized that his expression was strained and that he held his sword at a strange angle. It was as if two great stones hung invisibly in the air, and he was using his sword to lever them apart. It seemed that brute strength was holding open the angels' route into mortal London.

"Please." Rumiel sank toward the ground, his wings folding in behind him. "Listen to me. We have come to save you. To bring you back into the arms of righteousness."

"I've seen enough of your righteousness." Ines swung the knife around, pointing it directly at him. "You brought these people to Elizabeth's home, not to save us, but for the sake of your own power."

"For the sake of order. The sake of salvation." Rumiel was only yards away now, reaching out toward her. "Fair Ines, I mean only to protect you and your ilk."

"Get away from me!" she screamed, lunging at him with the knife. He dodged easily aside, and as she swiped at him, he rose into the air.

"I told you." Michael's voice was an avalanche rolling down upon her. "The children of Salgado are a menace, not allies to bind yourself to. They must be destroyed."

"She can be—"

"No." Michael winced and twisted his blade in the air, but his tone remained stern. "Rumiel, Sanctus, destroy them."

"With pleasure." Sanctus swung back his fist as he swept down toward Ines. Behind her, Toby whimpered in fear.

There was no time for calculation or clever plans. Ines saw one opening, and she used it.

Pulling back her arm, she flung her knife straight at Sanctus's face. As he ducked aside, she darted past him, bounded up onto a battered concrete bench, and leapt straight at Michael. The angel stared in surprise as she slammed into him. He must have weighed five times as much as her, and pain flared through her shoulder as she hit the plate armour encasing his body. In any other moment, it would have been a suicide attack, doing nothing more than causing him to stumble before he sliced her in half.

Here and now, that stumble was enough. As Michael jolted back a few inches, his blade lost its grip on the rip in reality it had held open. A wind swept through the marketplace as blackness opened in front of him, sucking the sword into its lightless depths. Yelling with rage, Michael was drawn in after it, and Sanctus with him. Rumiel was the last to vanish, and as Ines landed on the concrete slabs, she caught his gaze for a moment, seeing sadness there.

Then the angels were gone.

"Bugger me," Frank murmured. "I wasn't expecting that."

Ines looked at him and then at the piece of paper in Damon's hand.

"That had better be useful," she said, prodding at her bruised arm. "Because that really hurt."

CHAPTER 4
Comfort Food

Once upon a time, Ines had enjoyed spending time in cafes. They were relaxing places to go, somewhere you went for a treat. Whether it was going to a coffee shop with her dad, to be treated to a hot chocolate and cake, or sneaking out of school to spend the afternoon huddled over a can of cola in a local greasy spoon, they were places away from the strains of life and learning.

Not anymore. Now they were like miniature war rooms, places she went with Damon to plan their next move or to rest while on the run from hostile forces.

Places went with Damon and Rumiel, when they had been together.

"Here you go, love." The waitress plonked a plate down in front of Ines. "Full English and a can of Coke. And for you, sir"—she kept talking as she hurried back and forth from the counter—"full English with extra bacon and a lemonade."

Toby's eyes went wide at the plate she put in front of him. Cooked breakfasts were a rarity at home, and when they happened, they were usually part of their father's experimental cooking phases. A greasy fried breakfast with its heaps of meat, baked beans, runny egg, and fried bread still glistening from the pan—that was a holiday treat matched only by getting a fizzy drink at lunchtime.

"Brilliant." Toby looked up at Ines. "Do they have ketchup here?"

"Course we do, love." The woman placed another plate and a black coffee in front of Damon then fetched the brightly colored plastic sauce bottles off a neighbouring table. Ines kept a wary eye on her, watchful in case she should turn out to be a demon in disguise or a mage with plans for them. "Anything else I can get you?"

"No." Ines shook her head. "Thank you."

"Just shout if you want anything." Unbothered by Ines's sharp tone, the woman turned and waddled back to the counter, where more customers were waiting to be served.

"This is brilliant." Fragments of bacon flew as Toby spoke.

"Don't talk with your mouth full," Ines said.

"You're not Mum!" Toby glared.

"No, but she bought you lunch," Damon said calmly. "So stop behaving like a little dickhead and show some gratitude."

Toby hesitated, frozen between shame and defiance. At last he hung his head.

"Sorry." He put down his fork and sank his face into his hands. "I'm sorry. I didn't mean to be..."

Ines reached across the table and laid a hand on his shoulder.

"It's okay," she said.

"No, it isn't!" Toby looked up at her with tears in his eyes. "Those things were trying to kill you! And you fought that one with the sword. And the other one, he knew you, and he wanted to save you, and I don't understand, and I miss Dad, and I just..."

Ines stared uncertainly as he broke down sobbing into his hands. She glanced around and caught a sympathetic smile from the woman behind the counter. A nudge in the ribs made her look at Damon, who mimed a hug on the air in front of him.

Out of her depth but not wanting to let anyone down, Ines rose from the hard plastic seat and walked around the table, laying an arm around her brother.

"It'll be alright," she murmured, stroking his hair like she remembered her father doing when she was upset. "I promise, I'll look after you, and I'll find Mum and Dad."

Toby clung to her, his body shaking until it seemed there was no energy left in him. At last, he raised his head, wiped his eyes, and turned back to his meal.

"Thanks, Ines," he mumbled.

There was a long stretch of silence as she returned to her seat and they all focused on their meals. Fighting had made Ines hungry, Toby always had an appetite, and Damon seemed happy any time he was left to drink coffee. Ines noticed his concerned gaze flicking to her from time to time, and she tried to force a smile.

"Here, love." The waitress stood at the end of the table, holding out a magazine toward Toby. "Do you like cars?"

"They're alright." Toby shrugged and reached for the magazine. His smile was wobbly, but it was there. "Thank you."

"That's alright." The woman poured more coffee into Damon's mug and put another hot chocolate in front of Ines. "On the house. You deserve a treat for looking after your brother like that."

It was such a surprise to find random kindness in the world, after all the violence and horror she had seen, that Ines almost broke down in tears herself.

"Thank you so much," she whispered.

"That's alright." The waitress gathered their empty plates. "You take care now."

Watching her go, Ines sipped at the hot chocolate. It was cheap and watery, but the kindness of the gesture made it taste like the best thing in the world.

Damon slid his coffee into the middle of the table, making space in front of him. Then he spread out the piece of paper Frank had given him. The handwriting was so messy, it was illegible to Ines.

"It's the details of one of your mother's colleagues," Damon said. "Ann Magrs. Do you know her?"

"I've seen the name in the files," Ines said. "But Mum and Dad mostly kept work and colleagues away from us."

"Can you remember what the files said about Ann?" Damon picked up his coffee and did his best to lean back in his inflexible seat.

"She was listed as a specialist in research and knowledge gathering." Ines shook her head. "That's so vague, I just assumed it was code for something else. Is she some sort of magical secret agent?"

"The James Bond of the arcane inclined?" Damon gave a lopsided smile. "Hardly. Research and knowledge gathering is actually quite specific, once you realize those job titles are based on magical skills."

"Assume I don't know anything about magic," Ines said. "Because, as has been proved many times, I don't. What does this mean?"

"Every magic user is a specialist." Damon pulled the golden watch from his pocket. It dangled from the chain between his fingers, catching the white glare from the strip lights in the ceiling. "My magic comes from my father, so it's all about manipulating time. That can mean a lot of different things, depending on how I learn to use it, but it's what lets me freeze fights or dig around for information in someone's past, present, and future.

"Your mother and father were specialists in the magic of information. That can mean all sorts of things. It can mean research and information gathering, turning a mage into a top scholar in their field, able to provide insights and inventions no one else could ever come up with. It can be used to understand patterns in the world, both material and magical, to analyze the shifting nature of reality. It can be used for spying, though there are other magics that are better for that. And it can be about sending messages, reaching out to people without the usual communication methods or with a depth of understanding normal humans could never reach.

"It has its cost, just like any sort of magic, and that too depends on the mage. But what I've just described, those are the benefits."

"How does that help us find Mum and Dad?" Ines asked.

"Because of how your mother used her magic." Damon paused, looking thoughtfully at the piece of paper. "She was a researcher, highly focused, highly respected. I learnt that much from what I've seen in your study. In particular, she was an expert on arcane power and the relationships between the mortal and immortal realms."

"Relationships defined by the Barrier of Mercy." Ines leaned forward, squinting at the piece of paper, desperately trying to make sense of Frank's scrawl.

"Which explains why she was so important to Elizabeth Oldfield and her plans. It might also explain why they disagreed, though I don't know exactly how yet."

"You think Mum was taken because of this Ann woman?" Toby had set aside his magazine and was staring wide eyed at the note. Outside of exams, Ines had never seen a group of people so completely focused on a single piece of paper and the puzzle that lay within it.

"No." Damon folded up the note and put it back in his pocket. They all sat back, as if that gesture gave them permission to relax. "I think this is who she reached out to when she was attacked. Remember what my father said: the demons knew something was up because she sent out a distress call. I've talked with one of them since—not a pleasant conversation, dungworm demons stink worse than the school toilets—and there was part of the message they couldn't understand. Something that seemed garbled. Maybe it wasn't garbled. Maybe it was coded, and Ann Magrs would be able to understand that code."

"So we need to find her?" The information reinvigorated Ines. She had purpose again, a sense of direction that had been fading away. They had flailed around in the dark for so long, but now they had a beam of light to follow.

"Finding her will be easy." Damon grinned and pulled the paper back out of his pocket, waving it in front of her face. "We have her address. But you'd better pack a bag—we're going to Manchester."

* * *

A sense of unease settled over Ines as they left the cafe and walked down the street, heading toward the tube station. Something had snagged at the corner of her mind, and she trusted her instincts enough to try to make sense of it.

Trying not to be too obvious, she scanned the street ahead of them and to either side, looking for something that might have bothered her. Someone who glowed. The shadow of a demon seeping through into their world. Anything that might tell her what was wrong.

"We'll need food for the journey." She stopped outside a supermarket and gestured inside. "Pasties, sandwiches, stuff like that."

"Pork pie!" Toby hurried into the shop before anyone could change their mind. "And a cookie!" he called out once he was too far away to hear her say no.

Damon looked from Ines to the gleaming, well-stocked aisles with their bright packaging and clean white floor.

"We could make sandwiches at home," he said quietly. "We have to go there anyway before we head north."

A question hung unspoken in the air between them. It was almost a relief to Ines to know that she could be so transparent, that there was someone in the world who noticed when something bothered her.

"I've got a bad feeling." She took his arm and led him through the automatic doors. Once inside, she paused near the end of an aisle, turning them both to look at rows of snacks. The street outside was visible from the corner of her eye. "I think we're being followed."

"Shit." Damon made a show of choosing between two nearly identical packs of salt-and-vinegar crisps. "Angels again?"

"Not sure." Ines felt as if the world were closing in on her. She fought the urge to just stare out through the door. There were times when she needed to be subtle. Not every situation was one she could punch her way out of.

A gray shape walked slowly past the supermarket. A man in a suit, its cut and color so familiar, it was emblazoned across Ines's brain. For the briefest moment, he turned to look at them, and Ines turned away. The man kept walking, but a chill crawled up Ines's spine.

"Mages," she said. "The Ministry are watching us."

CHAPTER 5
Someone to Watch Over You

The streets were strangely quiet when they got off the tube. Barnet was seldom a bustling hive of activity, but it was still part of London, part of this urban sprawl crammed full of people. Midafternoon was closing time for the schools, most of which had reopened since the chaos and violence the breaking of the Barrier had unleashed. There should have been kids out and about in the streets, as well as the shoppers, workers, and old people who kept the local businesses ticking over during the day.

Hardly anyone walked along the pavement. Drivers rushed through with the intensity of those hounded by a

S.A. Beck

nightmare or a deadline. It was hardly a ghost town, but it wasn't normal.

Unsettling as the situation was, it worked for Ines. Without crowds to hide in, the man tailing them had to keep his distance, giving her more space to plan, more options to work with.

She wasn't going to be a victim of the schemes of others. Never again.

They stopped in front of an electronics shop and looked at the TVs in the window. The screens were all so large, there weren't many of them in the window. Ines had seen the TVs in old films and comics, little square boxes hardly bigger than her head. In those days, there would have been row upon row of TVs in the window. Out here in backwards Barnet, she felt as if that should still be the case. But of course no one bought those things anymore, and if they did, then the shops certainly wouldn't put them in a window display. Instead, there were a few gigantic flat screens, their colors bright and crisp to the point of unreality. Life just wasn't that crystal clear.

Three of the TVs were showing an animated film, trying to draw the attention of children and the parents with them.

Toby declared the film "too young" for him, even though Ines remembered him enjoying the same movie a year before.

The fourth screen was the interesting one. It was showing the news. Lines of police clashing with rioters, while a banner across the bottom announced the headlines.

"Rioting in Cambridge?" Ines blinked, half convinced the headline must be untrue. "What does anybody have to riot about in Cambridge?"

"Not getting a first in their degree?" Damon sneered. "A shortage of formal college dinners?"

"Do they eat a lot in Cambridge, then?" Toby asked.

Damon shook his head. "Fancy dinners. Cambridge is a fancy university town, the sort of place posh people go to get away from the rest of us."

"Mum and Dad went to Cambridge," Ines murmured. "That's where they met."

"Sorry." Damon's tone became reluctantly serious. "Being snarky is just my way of dealing."

"All right, Oprah." Ines offered him a smile. "I wasn't really offended. But still, why riot in Cambridge?"

Watching the screen, Damon spun his watch between his fingers.

"Traditional town," he said at last. "Lots of old churches, big thinkers, probably a theology Ministry. Exactly the sort of place that's vulnerable to angelic influences. And where the angels can get through, so can the demons. If we were there right now, I bet we'd see a dark throng hanging above those people's heads, and a choir two streets over singing for the holy horde."

His expression became distant as he spun the watch some more, twisting his fingers around it and mumbling under his breath. Ines stood to one side, blocking the view of him to anyone coming from the tube station. Tensed and ready, she waited for the first part of her plan to kick in.

The watch flashed, jerked, and went suddenly still.

"Alright, it's done." Damon slid the device back into his pocket. As he did so, Ines noticed blood trickling from the palm of his other hand.

"What did you do?" she asked.

"My magic needs suffering." Damon shrugged. "Now go, quick. I didn't have enough pain to hold him for long."

Ines sprinted back the way they had come. As she rounded a corner, she saw the man in the gray suit, standing in a spot Damon had picked out on their way past. He was frozen in mid-stride, not even breathing, time not passing, thanks to Damon's spell.

She grabbed the mage by the lapels of his suit just as the magic wore off. His body kept moving, even as his eyes went wide with surprise. With a simple judo move, Ines pulled him over her leg and down onto the ground then landed with her knee on his chest. He let out a pained grunt.

"You try anything like a spell, and I'll beat you senseless." Ines balled her fist and held it over her head.

"I'm not scared of some little girl." The mage started to move his fingers in arcane arcs.

Ines slammed her fist into his nose, blood spraying from the impact. Then she grabbed one of his hands, twisting back two fingers until they gave way with a sickening snap.

"I'm not a little girl," she said. "Not anymore. Now tell me why you're following us, or I'll finish off that hand and get started on the other one."

"All right, all right!" The mage's voice was bubbly and wavering. With his dark glasses knocked off, Ines could make out hazel eyes. He might have been handsome once, but age and her fist had seen the end of that. "We're under orders from Minister Oldfield."

"Minister Oldfield now, is she?" Ines raised her fist again. "Since when?"

"Since all hell started breaking loose. They needed someone with real magical understanding at the top."

"She caused that chaos!"

"It wasn't meant to be this way." He glared. "It would have been different, if not for you."

Slapping him wasn't even a conscious decision. It was just something Ines's hand did, a venting of her hatred against his.

"Why follow us?" she growled.

"Why do you think?" he spat. "To keep you from fucking things up again."

Ines slapped him once more, deliberately and forcefully.

"I caught you—I can catch whoever else you send." From what she'd seen of the Ministry mages, she had her doubts, but this was no time to let them show. "You tell Oldfield I'm coming for my parents, and nothing she does will stop that."

She slammed her fist into his face. There was a thud of his head against the concrete, and he went limp.

Looking up, she saw Toby staring at her with horrified fascination, Damon with a grim look behind him. A few passersby had also stopped to stare, and one had her phone out.

"We should go," Ines said. "Whatever you're going to say can wait."

* * *

"What have I done?" Ines sat on the edge of her bed, head in her hands. "I just beat someone senseless in front of Toby. That's... He shouldn't see that!"

Damon closed the door softly behind him and went to sit beside her on the bed. Pictures of film stars and martial artists stared down at him, an intruder in a space usually reserved for them and Ines.

"The world's a dark place," he said. "Toby would be far worse off if you let the Ministry get to him. Heck, without you, he'd still be their prisoner."

"Mum and Dad hid this stuff from me." Ines stared down at the bloodstains on her hands. How had she not washed them off yet? She tried to will herself to go do it but couldn't find the strength to get up off the bed. "I can't even fix him decent meals or get him to go to bed on time."

Damon put his arm tentatively around her. She leaned into him, resting her head on his shoulder.

"Some days, I barely feel like I can take care of myself," she said. "How can I look after Toby, never mind do that while finding Mum and Dad?"

"Are you kidding?" Damon brushed back a loose strand of her hair. "You're the strongest person I know. You're keeping Toby safe and happy, even with all the craziness that's going on. There are people out there fighting in the streets, vanishing into themselves, or losing their grip on the world. And here's you, a sixteen-year-old, making your brother feel like most days are just another day off school. Sure, today was bad. But compared with what's on the TV? At least he knows he's safe around you."

Ines turned to him with a smile.

"How do you always know what to say?" she asked.

"Part genius, part too many books." He smiled back. "So I'm thinking you could do with a rest before we head north. I'll cook us some dinner, you can get cleaned up, and—"

"No." Ines forced herself to her feet. If she stayed like this, comfortable and comforted, sat beside Damon in her room, then she might never get up again. The only way to keep going was exactly that— to keep going, whenever and however she could. "We head up to Manchester tonight. Toby's packing his bag already, and you've got your overnight stuff in the living room."

She pulled a sports bag out from under her bed then paused, looking around to decide what she should take. She had no idea how long they might be away, but they needed to travel light. A few clothes, wash kit, and whatever weapons she needed to fight demons.

Emergency chocolate. There was no way she'd get through the next week without that. Opening a drawer in her desk, she pulled out a box and tipped its brightly wrapped contents into her bag. Not just for her, she told herself. For Toby too.

As she glanced up, she saw a serious expression on Damon's face. Was he going to try to talk her down, to make her stay and look after herself? That was exactly the sort of thing he would come out with, the sort of thing that made him so great to have around.

Exactly the sort of thing she couldn't stand to hear right now.

"You said all the mages are special-ists." It was the first thing that came to mind, a way of filling the silence before he could. "What do those Ministry stooges specialize in?"

"Nothing that matters to their job." Damon stood uncertainly and went over to the doorway, looking away as she rifled through her underwear drawer. "I mean, the specialization is relevant, but it's not the point. Ministry enforcers are trained in combat magic and spells designed to counter supernatural forces. It's a tough regime to follow, one that's been built up over the centuries. It lets them reliably channel magic of different styles and origins into something for fighting strange creatures."

"So what they're good at gets beaten out of them, turning them into magical soldiers?" She grabbed a pair of jogging pants out of the wardrobe and flung them into her bag. "That's horrible."

"It's not quite as simple as that." Damon scratched his head. "Again, the metaphors don't quite work. They pick mages who are suited to the work, whose magic will fit with it. And later on, when they get promoted or retire from front-line service, then they get to focus more on their own sorts of magic."

"So they aren't just identikit stormtroopers?" Ines asked.

"Only part time." Damon gave a half smile. The watch was spinning in his fingers again, nervous energy going into practicing movements for when he'd need them.

"How comforting." Ines zipped her bag shut.

With a shrug, Damon stood and walked over to her, resting a hand on her shoulder.

"Ines, you need to look after yourself," he said. "There's no point saving the world if you destroy yourself along the way."

"If I can save my family in the process, then there is." She ducked beneath the hand, around him, and out the door. "Come on, we've got a train to catch."

CHAPTER 6
Strangers at the Station

It was strange how easily people could act as if everything were normal. The news was full of trouble from all over the country—outbreaks of crime and disorder from Lands End to John O'Groats. Euston station itself still bore the scars of London's recent difficulties. Black stains marked where fires had burned up the picnic tables outside the station building, and several of the shops that flanked the concourse were smashed in, metal shutters tangled, signs reduced to fragments of brightly colored plastic.

Yet, in the midst of this carnage, people were going about their business as if nothing had changed. Commuters in suits; tourists peering at maps of the city; shoppers out for the day, diving into the Tube station or staring at the board listing local trains. All acted as if everything were perfectly normal—or as normal as it could get inside the concrete box of a modern train station.

"Is it a particularly British thing, do you think?" Ines watched a man stride past in the pinstripe suit and forced confidence of an investment fund manager. The volume with which he shouted into his phone perfectly matched his swift, intense stride. "Do people in other countries react when they see things go to hell? Change their lives, leave the country, at least stop going about their ordinary days?"

"I doubt it." Damon sat across the table from her. They had found seats at the edge of a food court inside the station building. Half a dozen catering concessions lurked around them like branded and well-fed vultures, smells of coffee and toasted panini coming from every one. The tables, seats, and fixtures had the same identikit forced-casual style of so many coffee shops and chain bars across the city. The biggest difference was that this place was crammed full at half past three in the afternoon.

"People are people, the world over." Damon sipped thoughtfully at a black coffee. "They don't like to acknowledge change. There might be a demon eating babies in the next seat over, but if they can get away with ignoring it and living in peace, then they will."

"Do demons really eat babies?" Toby stared wide eyed from behind an over-priced cookie.

"Some of them." Damon put on a mischievous grin. "Personally, I prefer to eat twelve-year-olds."

"I'm not scared of you." Toby folded his arms. "Besides, Ines will protect me."

"Maybe I'll get hungry too." She shrugged, trying to enjoy the moment even as her gaze kept flicking to the departures board. She would be a lot more comfortable once they were on a train and heading north, away from the people who wanted to make her life hell—in some cases literally.

"Speaking of demons." Damon let out a long sigh. "Here comes trouble."

A spindly figure was making its way through the crowd, its steps so erratic, they barely counted as walking. At first glance, it could be taken as human, and Ines presumed that was what most people saw, but to her, it was clearly something else. Its black suit hung in irregular folds from limbs so angular and stick thin that they could have been made of broomsticks. Beneath the sort of wide-brimmed hat favored by orthodox Jews and dedicated Lord of the Rings fans, a spiked nose protruded above two rows of blackened, jagged teeth. An unconvincing layer of something that was meant to look like skin hung, pale and misshapen, from whatever passed for a face beneath that facade.

The creature lurched up to the coffee counter. As it passed them, one bulbous green eye gave Damon an exaggerated wink.

The youth behind the counter stood frozen for a moment, staring at the apparition before him. Then his expression shifted as habit took hold, and his brain told him not only that he must be looking at a fellow human being, but also that it was rude to gawp at the disfigurement of others. At the creature's request, he served up a triple espresso, handing over the tiny cup in exchange for a handful of grimy coins.

"Keep the change," the demon hissed.

It approached their table with the same strange walk that had carried it across the station, as if it were swinging its weight from one leg to the other, unable to control the way those legs settled beneath it. It fell into the fourth chair like a puppet whose strings had been suddenly cut, somehow keeping its coffee upright through the whole endeavour.

"Viscount Demi-Chron." Fingers like needles grasped the top of the creature's hat and lifted it a few inches in greeting. As it did so, Ines caught a glimpse of knotted, greasy hair as pale as its skin. The huge eyes seemed to fill its entire forehead.

"So now I'm a Viscount?" Damon took another sip of his coffee. His expression was muted, but Ines saw a flicker of anger in his eyes. "Good for me. If I keep getting promoted for staying away from my father, I'll soon be Emperor of the World."

"The power is yours, if you so choose." The demon looked at Ines and Toby. "It is a matter of priorities."

Damon pushed his cup away and leaned forward, letting the anger seize his whole face.

"I'm not in the mood for extensive bullshit, Eldervain." He glared at the demon. "So save us all the more-evil-than-thou posing and the menacing insinuations. Why has my father sent you here?"

"Can't I just be looking out for the beloved child of my lord and master?" Eldervain blinked, heavy lids large and slow.

"You don't even know what beloved means. Cut the crap—I have a train to catch."

"Very well." Eldervain reached inside its jacket. There was a ripping sound, and then it dropped something on the table.

Ines peered at the object. It was the size and shape of a marble, black as death and dripping with something just as dark. The polish on the wooden surface fizzled and charred as the ooze hit it, and a trickle of heavy gray smoke drifted from the table down to the floor.

Damon stared at it in shock then back at Eldervain.

"This is just a beginning," the demon said. "Your father offers you power beyond measure. Power second only to his own. Power that in time may even exceed his. He takes pride in your rebellion—after all, who are Lucifer's children to reject the prodigal son? He wishes to assure you that all that is his, all that Hell can make manifest, is yours for the taking."

The clatter of teacups and rumble of wheeled luggage continued around them. At the table, nobody spoke, while above them, the departures board counted in the trains and listed the destinations of those still to come.

"Well?" Eldervain waved at the black ball, which had ceased dripping and smoking. "It is freely given, and I know enough of what passes to know that you have need of the power." He grinned. "With this, next time, you could really make that cockroach Michael regret threatening your friends."

Damon sank back into his seat.

"Go," he said, his voice quiet but hard as stone. "Take it. I want no part of this power."

"So sad, this rift in your family." Eldervain stood. It was like watching an origami crane unfold. "I leave this with you, lest you should reconsider. Your father's door lies open, and his power is yours even should you not return. Do not forget who you are, Viscount Demi-Chron."

"That's Damon." He stood and raised his voice as the creature staggered away, shouting to be heard above the commuter crowds. "My name is Damon!"

A dozen people turned to look at him as he sank, red faced, back into his seat. Then they all looked away, scurrying on about their business.

"I thought you were trying to blend in," said a voice behind Ines.

She turned with a start to see a woman in a gray suit looking at them from the next table.

"How long have you been there?" Ines asked. "Don't come any closer. I've beaten you before—I can do it again."

"No need for alarm." Tamsin Shaw took off her dark glasses, revealing pale-blue eyes beneath a short blond bob. "If I were here to arrest you, we wouldn't be talking now."

Ines turned her seat and slid a hand inside the backpack she held under the table, fingers closing around the handle of a knife. She didn't like hurting human beings, and the last time she faced Shaw, she had been able to avoid doing her any serious harm. But, the last time, Damon had empowered Ines by placing his magic on her fists. She doubted he would want to do that again.

"Make it quick," Ines said. "We have a train to catch."

"So I see." Shaw raised an eyebrow. "Where to, I wonder? Manchester? Liverpool? Birmingham? Or are you fleeing to some out-of-the-way corner of the countryside? You wouldn't be the only one—several members of the cabinet have decided that's the safest option. Which goes to show how smart politicians aren't."

"This is you being quick?" Damon stood beside Ines, gold watch dangling from his hand. "It seems like stalling to me."

"Heaven forbid I should create a poor impression on you, Mr. Lorus," Shaw said. "Though, judging by that last conversation, Heaven won't be forbidding you anything for long."

She stood, walked around, and settled into the seat previously occupied by Eldervain. As she did so, Ines noticed that the black ball had gone from the table.

"You two are important," Shaw said. "You defied the Ministry once, and you're clearly still plotting something— otherwise, you would be in hiding. But you have to know that you can't win. We have most of the mages in Britain at our disposal, and all of the best. We have contacts in the police and security services. We have all the resources that a government Ministry can bring to bear, and even in the age of austerity, that is a lot of resources. However far you run, however hard you fight, however cunningly you hide, we'll get you in the end.

"This is your chance to come peace- fully. In two minutes' time, I'm going to get up from this table and walk away. No tricks, no traps, no ambushes—I'll just be heading back to the Ministry. Come with me, and you can surrender without anyone else getting hurt. We can talk about what has been troubling you. We'll find a safe, comfortable place for your brother to stay. You'll even get to see your parents."

"You have Mum and Dad?" Toby's expression was desperate in its longing. It tugged at Ines's heartstrings. Going with Shaw felt like the only thing she could do.

But, however she felt, she also knew that the Ministry couldn't be trusted.

"Get bent." She stood and slung her bag over her shoulder. "We have a train to catch."

With Damon and Toby in tow, she stomped away from the table, across the station, under the departures board, and toward the platform advertising a high-speed train to Manchester. Nearing the platform entrance, she risked a glance back. Shaw was gone.

"Well done." Damon gripped her hand, and his touch stilled the shaking that had taken hold of her.

"Need the loo," Toby said as they approached the ticket barrier.

"Fine." Ines sighed. "We'll wait here."

As Toby hurried off, she turned to face Damon.

"Thanks for having my back there," she said.

"Always." He bent close, moving in to kiss her. Her hand tightened around his at the thrill of his lips against hers. "You know, I think I've loved you exactly as long as I've known you."

"That's..." She hesitated, unsure what to think or feel. In the moment of the kiss, she had felt a rush of happiness, but now she hesitated. Was this what she wanted? Even if it was, was now the time?

She didn't resist as Damon kissed her again, their lips locking in shared passion, detached for a moment from the chaos of their lives.

Then they separated, Ines untangling her fingers from his and catching her breath before Toby could return. On the platform, a train waited to carry them north.

CHAPTER 7
Judgment

Their carriage was almost empty, only a few other passengers scattered up and down the aisles. They found a free table and slid into the seats around it, Damon sitting next to Ines, Toby opposite them. As he sat, Damon's hand brushed against Ines's. She moved to take a chocolate bar out of her bag, breaking the contact rather than decide whether it was what she wanted.

After a few minutes, the doors hissed shut, the train shuddered, and they began their journey north. Outside the windows, the bright lights of Euston station turned briefly into dark tunnels then the backs of houses and graffiti-strewn concrete embankments as they accelerated out of London. The tracks took them almost the same way they had come into the city on the Tube, but without descending into the ground, they got to see the city fly by. The towering modern blocks of office buildings gave way to recent housing developments, new flats in bricks of a soft orange brown. Then came rows of older terraces, interspersed with the concrete behemoths of 1960s housing estates, with only the occasional neglected park or school field to provide a touch of greenery.

The train rattled and swayed as they finally emerged into open countryside, traveling far faster than the ageing Tube trains could manage. This was a modern machine, decked out in the red-and-purple livery of one of the companies that ran the rails. A smiling attendant pushed past them with a cart full of snacks and drinks, and Damon bought another coffee.

"How much of that stuff can one man drink?" Ines looked at the steaming cardboard cup.

"It's something to do." Damon shrugged. "Besides, if we're facing some kind of apocalypse, then I'd like to enjoy the journey there."

"Manchester's the apocalypse now?" Ines grinned.

"It might as well be." Damon rolled his eyes. "What of value could exist beyond London, with its perfect streets and its oh-so-charming residents."

"London isn't that great." Toby looked surprised.

"Sarcasm, mate." Damon shook his head. "Get used to it. You'll use it a lot once you grow up."

"I'm not a little kid." Toby glared. "I'll show you."

Showing them consisted of taking an iPhone out of his bag and plugging himself into it. Tinny beats emerged from the earbuds, joining the rattle of the train in a staccato soundtrack to their journey.

Watching fields, trees, and roads roll by, Ines contemplated what lay ahead of them. It didn't seem as if the Ministry would take no for an answer, especially as she intended to go poking around in their business. Nor were the angels likely to leave them in peace now they were outside the safety of the city. As they passed through towns, she caught glimpses of glowing forms hovering above cars, houses, and passersby. Unnatural shadows skulked in the human landscape, horns raised and claws extended. The hosts of Hell were on the prowl.

"That thing Eldervain gave you." She spoke quietly, hoping that Toby wouldn't hear them over his music. "What was that?"

"Temptation," Damon replied. He hesitated, blowing on his cup to cover for the delay. "There are many ways a demon can learn to harness more power. They don't come through studying, like they do for mages. It's more about seizing opportunities, showing your strength and brutality by grasping what others want. But it can be about patronage too, reinforcing the hierarchy of the damned through gifts from lords to their minions."

"Or from a father to his son?" Ines fought the urge to reach out and lay a hand on his. There was another conversation down that path, one she definitely didn't want to have in front of Toby.

"Yes." Damon's tone was sharp with anger.

"Sorry," Ines said. That voice stung. "I just meant..."

"I know." Damon sighed. "It's just... None of this is easy for me either, you know?"

He looked up and tensed.

"Trouble coming." He popped the plastic lid onto his coffee and slid it to one side.

A door at the far end of the carriage had opened, and a woman was walking toward them. She seemed ordinary enough in herself, with her swaying skirts and long, curly hair. The smile with which she greeted the world was wide to the point of unsettling, but Ines wasn't going to judge someone for enjoying herself.

Especially not when supernatural forces were meddling in that pleasure.

An angel drifted along behind the woman, its feet six inches off the floor. It didn't have the warlike stance of Michael and his kin, nor the solidity that made Rumiel so achingly human. It looked as if a life-size doll had been woven from strands of light and smoke, forming the outline of a body but leaving it half empty. Its glow lit up the carriage, and the air shimmered in its wake, but she could see through it to the wall beyond. Its long fingers lay on the woman's shoulders, gently massaging her as she walked.

"Peace and love." The woman took a tulip from a basket and laid it in the lap of the first passenger she passed. He looked up at her in confusion then smiled as the angel reached out and, unseen by him, brushed his forehead with its glowing hand.

"Peace and love," the woman said as she dropped a flower in the lap of the next passenger. "Peace and love. Peace and love."

It was an unsettling sight to watch. The beauty of the angel and the kindness of the woman's actions made joy rise in Ines's heart. But she knew that this was a symptom of a wider disease afflicting the country—of angelic armies and demonic hordes, of chaos, turmoil, and death. How long before even this moment of kindness turned into one of disaster, the woman stepping in front of a car in her blissed-out state, or straight out the door of the speeding train?

"Peace and—"

"Love, yes, I get it." Damon grabbed the flower as she held it out, ushering her on with a wave of his hand. But if he had hoped to keep the angel moving, paying them no attention, it was already too late.

The creature looked at them with eyes as wide as a cartoon kitten's.

"Rumiel is looking for you." Its voice was like warm honey. "He will be so pleased to hear that you are here."

They stared in horror as the angel floated on up the train.

"Can we stop it?" Ines asked.

"Not unless you know how," Damon said. "Do you think we should get off at the next stop, before it can call the pompous host down upon us?"

Ines shook her head.

"What would be the point?" she said. "We'd only have to get to Manchester some other way, and they'd probably spot us on the roads. We're halfway there already, and there's no faster way than this train. We just have to hope that we can get there before something terrible arrives."

Reaching inside her bag, she pulled out a kitchen knife and laid it on her knees underneath the table. She felt like a psycho killer out of a Hollywood movie, waiting armed and patiently for her victim to arrive. But though the image made her blood run cold, she was determined to be ready for whatever came.

Without a word, Damon got out of his seat and went to sit on the far side of the table, placing himself between Toby and the aisle. Ines shuffled over so that she was facing him. Between the two of them, they could see anyone approaching, whichever way they came down the carriage.

They waited like that, not a word passing between them, as the train hurtled along its tracks, across the Midlands and into the north. Ines wasn't sure if it was her imagination or if the sky really looked more gray out here. Damon sipped at his cold coffee, eyes fixed on the door, while she drummed her fingers on the flat of the knife.

"I feel sick." Toby had taken out his headphones and was looking plaintively at Ines.

"It's probably motion sickness." She could feel a little of it in her own belly, unused to travelling on such a swiftly swaying train. "Don't worry, we're nearly there."

Over an hour out of London, the train started making its few stops before Manchester. People got out of the coach, and no more got on board. Soon there was only one other passenger, a man in a well-kept leather jacket who sat tapping at a laptop.

"Next stop: Manchester Piccadilly." The sign scrolled past above the door, dots of light forming the letters against a black background.

Allowing herself a moment of relief, Ines sank back in her chair.

"Ten more minutes." She smiled at Toby. "Don't worry, we can get off the train soon, and I'll get you a ginger beer. That's supposed to be good for upset stomachs."

"Yuck!" Toby stuck out his tongue. "I remember that ginger tea Dad made. I'm not touching that stuff." His grimace turned to a frown. "I miss Dad."

"That's OK, we'll find him soon." Ines took his hand, but he was twelve years old, too mature in his own mind for such public gestures, and he jerked back. "And then we'll—"

The words froze in her throat. A golden glow was shining through the glass at the end of the carriage. The door hissed open, and Rumiel stepped through.

He smiled at them, a wide, open smile, like a child presented with the beauty of a rainbow. In his hand was a sword, and blood dripped from the blade.

The man working at his laptop looked up with a small frown, as if a fly had buzzed across his vision. But the distraction faded, his mind unable to comprehend what it was seeing, filing the angel away as simply not there. Something of Rumiel's glory had rubbed off on him, though, and as he returned smiling to his work, he typed faster than before.

Rumiel paused as he passed the man and laid a hand on his shoulder.

"Simon Dalton." Rumiel's voice was clear as the tolling of a church bell. "You have done wrong. You have neglected your duty to the Lord God. You have blasphemed, and you have shown cruelty to those around you. You shall feel the weight of your sins."

The man's face went green. He buckled over, vomiting all over himself and his computer. Whimpering, he clutched his stomach in pain.

Ines gagged at the sudden stench of vomit, and Toby turned pale.

"After this ordeal, if you find the path of righteousness, then you may be saved," Rumiel announced. "If not..."

The tip of his sword rested for a moment on Simon Dalton's shoulder, an inch from the arteries in his throat.

"Ines." Rumiel smiled as he approached them. "I was so pleased to hear that you were here. That you have emerged from the stain of London and come forth into this world of the righteous."

"Get up," Ines said to the other two.

Rising from her seat, she slung the bag over her shoulder, while with her other hand she held out the knife, its point twinkling in the golden glow of Rumiel's presence. She took a few steps toward him, placing herself between the angel and her companions.

Outside the windows, fields had given way to redbrick terraces and railway sidings. They passed through a station, concrete pillars holding rainswept roofs up above grim platforms.

"Stay away from me." She backed down the train, knife still outstretched.

"But Ines." Rumiel held his arms wide. "I only want to save you. And for us to be together. Don't you want that too?"

His smile was hypnotic. She found herself gazing at him, time sliding by with the stations as the warmth of his presence filled her blood. He seemed more powerful than before and even more beautiful. She felt safe and protected. Her mind filled with images of how perfect life could be if she gave in to his will.

"Ines." Damon's hand on her shoulder snapped her back to reality.

Blinking back the images, she saw that the train was coming into another station, larger than any of the others they had passed.

"Manchester Piccadilly," a voice said over the speakers. "All change here. All change."

The train ground to a halt, and the doors swept open. Sliding her knife out of sight, Ines ushered the others out onto the platform.

Rumiel stopped in the doorway, staring past them at the hundreds of bustling people. He took a deep breath, like a hunting dog sniffing the breeze.

"So many to be judged," he said. "So much good work to be done." His gaze returned to Ines. "But don't worry, I will still come for you."

The words echoed in Ines's ears as she turned and ran.

CHAPTER 8
Tea and Talons

At first, Manchester wasn't at all like Ines expected. Everything she knew about the city came from history lessons or her dad's eclectic record collection. Between them, they offered two visions of Manchester—one of desolate Victorian slums, tight redbrick terraces full to over-crowding with poor people and disease, the other of a modern center full of clubs and arenas, mop-haired guitarists picking fights with top-flight DJs in front of crowds of lager-fueled fans. It was the home of industrialism and a peculiarly British version of rock and roll, its glamor replaced with rough belligerence.

Instead, she dashed out of the station and into a world of modern office blocks and towering hotels, receding to the battered shop fronts and open gardens of Piccadilly. Even the tram they leapt on, and which her phone assured her would take her to Ann Magrs's part of town, was newer, brighter, and cleaner than she'd expected. Of course, there were misguided chunks of sixties architecture, the odd tramp begging for change with a Starbucks cup, and tired-looking office workers smoking on street corners. This was still Britain, after all.

"What did you expect" Damon laughed at her expression of surprise. "It's not like we've fled to Uzbekistan or Milton Keynes."

"I just..." She watched a collection of new flats shoot past the window, then a line of bars and corner shops. At last, she gave an embarrassed grin. "I guess I've just never spent much time outside of London."

The tram rattled to a stop, and its doors clunked open.

"Here we are." Damon took the lead, phone in hand, following the directions on his screen. A few drops of rain spattered their coats, and Ines pulled up her hood, making sure not to bring it so far forward, it would block her peripheral vision. If there was trouble, then she wanted to see it coming.

They soon found themselves on a street of red brick Victorian housing, the road lined with cars parked halfway onto the pavement. A few trees lined the road, though the stumps of others stood testament to the ravages of age and drunk drivers. The houses weren't exactly the vision of Manchester in Ines's head—if nothing else, the semi-detached dwellings were far larger than those of the Victorian slum etchings—but they were enough like that image to bring a smile to her lips.

At the end of the street, a couple were arguing. A dark shape hung, ephemeral and drifting like smoke, above their heads. A demon was on its way.

"Let's get on with this." Ines marched up the half dozen stone steps to Ann Magrs's porch and rang the doorbell. A chime like ancient bells, cracked yet beautiful, came to her through the clouded glass.

"Just coming!" Footsteps followed the voice down the hall, and a moment later, the door opened. "How can I help?"

Ann Magrs was nothing like the Ministry mages Ines had met so far. Dressed in a loose woollen jumper and baggy floral-print pants, she stood before them in bare feet, a small black cat held lovingly in the fold of one arm. Her hair was a wild mass of curls, hanging around a beaming smile and a pair of glasses with thick plastic frames.

"My name is Ines Salgado." Ines held out her hand. "Julie's daughter. I was hoping—"

"Quick, quick, get inside!" Ann ushered them in then peered up and down the street before slamming the door shut. The tension that had briefly held her vanished as she shut out the world. "Good good. Good good. Let's make tea. We should talk."

* * *

Ann Magrs's house was beyond eclectic. Every surface of the walls was covered with drawings, maps, and diagrams, some of them framed, others pinned or stuck up with sticky tack. Vast padded armchairs filled the living room, three of them occupied by fat, fluffy cats. In the kitchen, a selection of mismatched wooden chairs surrounded a table whose polished surface had been scarred by years of mug rings and the indentations of ballpoint pens. Even the ceiling was crowded, a selection of large-print recipes hanging above their heads and a clothes-line stretching from corner to corner of the room. It was strangely comforting, and Ines wondered if this was how her dad would have lived without her mum to assert some order.

"Here." Ann placed a bright-blue teapot in the middle of the table, together with a milk bottle and a selection of mugs.

"Thank you." Taking the least-cracked cup, Ines poured herself a drink. She wasn't very fond of tea, but it seemed polite. "I think maybe you know why we're here?"

"Oh yes." Ann grabbed a pile of papers from the sideboard and dumped them in the middle of the table. "I've been trying to make sense of it this whole time, but you know Julie, so smart, so secretive. The key could be almost anything."

"Key?" Ines set her mug down and reached for Ann's hand. "Please, can you just sit down and start from the beginning? We're confused, we don't know much about Mum's work, and for the past few weeks, we've just been struggling to stay alive. We may need the simple version."

"Simple version." Ann nodded and absentmindedly petted the cat that leapt up onto her knee. "Of course. Let me think... You say you don't know much about your mother's work? But you know about the Barrier of Mercy?"

"We've had to learn fast." Ines gestured to Damon and Toby, who were quietly drinking their own tea while trying to fend off the attention of the cats. "And its effects have been hard to miss lately."

"Indeed." Ann started rifling through the papers. "We're the Ministry's top experts on the Barrier, Julie and I. Your mother and I, that is. Elizabeth knows a lot, of course, and David has picked up bits and pieces just from being around us."

"You mean Elizabeth Oldfield?"

"Oh, yes, of course. And David Salgado. Your father." Ann turned a fond smile on Toby and, much to his disgruntlement, ruffled his hair. "You look so much like him."

"S'pose." Toby looked away, deciding to pay attention to a kitten nibbling at his jeans.

Outside, a police siren screeched by. Ann frowned, her face crumpling like an old tissue.

"It's been getting worse this week." She pulled out a pile of printouts from news pages. "I have the statistics, but it can be hard to get the police to listen to an old hippy. And of course I can't go to the Ministry now."

"Why not?" Damon asked. "Surely you're still one of them?"

Ann's snort would have put a pig to shame.

"That very much depends upon who you mean by them. I was never one of Elizabeth's favorites, however much she tried to flatter me in the past few months. I should have known that something was wrong then, that she was taking too active an interest. She would call asking questions about my work, strange things, specific things. Silly old bag that I am, I took it as a compliment. Now I know better."

"You said something about a key?" Ines backtracked through the tangle of conversation. She wanted answers she could understand, but she wanted them on Ann's terms. That way she stood a better chance of learning what was really important, not just the things that seemed relevant to an outsider like her.

"To the code." Ann glanced at the pile of papers and rolled her eyes. "Honestly, I'll never find it this way."

Closing her eyes, the mage flung the papers into the air, letting them scatter like giant snowflakes. Mumbling something under her breath, she reached out with one hand, fingers glowing with a spiderweb of light. Two sheets of paper drifted toward her through the tumbling mass, clinging to her glowing hand. She opened her eyes, spread the sheets out on the table in front of them, and weighed the corners down with mugs and the milk bottle.

The papers were computer printouts, one crowded with apparently random letters and numbers, the other carrying a single simple message:

"Oldfield is breaching the Barrier of Mercy. You have to stop her. I have been..." There the message ended.

"Julie and I had been working on an interface that allowed us to electronically capture the contents of communication spells." Ann pointed at the more garbled of the two sheets. "It allowed the sending of deeply encoded information, and the application of electronic cryptography to mystical signals." She patted Toby's head again. "That part was David's idea."

"So this is in code?" Ines asked.

"Of course," Ann said. "Though, without the key, it is impossible to decode."

"Cool." Toby peered at the paper. "It's like in spy films. There's probably a computer program that'll decode it, and it's hidden in a basement somewhere. There'll be lasers and those fingerprint locks."

"No, no." Ann shook her head. "We hadn't managed to master the electronic cryptography side yet—it's too unreliable. This will be mystical—a code phrase or spell whose recitation will decipher the message."

"What's it about?" The paper had Toby's interest now. Ines was pleased to see him enjoying something other than eating or reading his glossy magazines, but the thought of involving him more deeply in the situation worried her.

"I don't know." Ann pushed her glasses up her nose. "Perhaps more information about Elizabeth's plans, or something about the barrier. Maybe a message about what was happening to Julie. I assume she intended to tell me, and to send a clue to the key, but someone cut her off."

"How very perceptive of you, Magrs." A cold, hard voice came from the hallway.

Leaping to her feet, Ines snatched a knife from the improvised sheath of packing tape hidden up her sleeve. She leapt into position between the table and the door, blade held in front of her.

Elizabeth Oldfield walked into the room as if she owned it. Her head was held high, blond hair drawn back from her stately features.

"Give me the message." She held out a hand. She could hardly have looked more out of place, her pinstripe suit ill fitting with the gentle clutter of Ann Magrs's home.

"No." Magrs rose, thrust the papers into Damon's hand, and walked around to stand beside Ines. The carefree hippy was gone, replaced by a woman just as focused in her own way as Oldfield. "This is my house, Elizabeth, and I have been preparing for this moment. Do you think you can demand anything of me in my place of power?"

"Alone? No." Oldfield's eyes flickered, as bright and deadly looking as the gold lion pin on her lapel. "But do you think your feeble fortress of the mind can stand against the power of the Ministry?"

Footsteps in the corridor announced the arrival of more mages, Tamsin Shaw among them, all in their matching gray suits and sunglasses.

"I think you should be going now, children." Ann raised her hands in front of her, glowing letters and numbers spiraling around them. "There's a gate at the bottom of the garden. Quick as you can."

"Damon, take Toby." Ines gestured toward the back door then turned back to face Oldfield. "I'll catch up."

To her relief, the sound of the door showed that the boys could listen. That gave her one less thing to worry about.

She raised her knife.

The mages advanced, ghostly glowing clubs appearing in their right hands, shields on the left. All except Elizabeth. As she took a fighting stance, her hands disappeared, turning into furred paws that ended in razor-sharp claws. The cats clustered at her feet, turning on their owner with an angry hiss.

"Get them," Elizabeth growled.

Two of the mages swept past her. The kitchen, which had seemed spacious for four of them sat down to tea, felt like a tiny place for a desperate fight.

With one hand, Ines held out the knife, using it to fend off her attacker. With the other, she reached back and grabbed the teapot off the table. She didn't want to stab another human being if she could avoid it, and there weren't many real weapons at hand.

The mage attacked with his club. She ducked, spun left, and swung the teapot at his head. He parried just in time to stop the blow, and the teapot shattered. Scalding-hot liquid spattered his face, and he closed his eyes, yelling with pain. Not giving him a moment to recover, Ines punched him in the stomach, doubling him over, and then turned to face the rest.

Ann Magrs clearly fought using her specialty, not the brute magic of the Ministry. The weapons of one gray-suited mage were caught in a tangle of glowing letters, while two others had slumped to the floor, strange symbols dancing before eyes that had gone blank with bewilderment.

"Go, go," Ann snapped. "I can hold them on my own. Someone needs to find your parents."

Ines ran, even as more mages emerged from the corridor. This time, Oldfield was in the lead, claws outstretched. As Ines dashed out of the doorway, the minister leapt at Ann Magrs, who flung her arms wide, summoning papers and cookbooks from around the room in a protective barrier. There was a tearing sound, an angry cry, and then a scream.

Turning at the garden gate, Ines glanced back through the kitchen window. Elizabeth Oldfield stood amid a flurry of flying papers. Her face was spattered with blood, and more dripped from her claws. Behind her, Tamsin Shaw stood wide eyed with shock, staring at the torn face of Ann Magrs as the information mage slumped against the wall and then slid to the floor, blood pouring from her throat.

CHAPTER 9
Dealing With Toby

Heart pounding, Ines ran across the playing field behind Ann Magrs's house. Damon and Toby stood by a gate on the far side of the field, the older boy with his hand on Toby's shoulder, those two precious sheets of paper clutched in his hand.

It was late in the day, but there were still people out and about, a group of teenagers laughing and smiling as they played football in the last light of dusk, the faint glow of an angel hovering above their heads. As Ines ran through the middle of their game, they turned and shouted to her to join in, their expressions shifting to bewilderment and fear as they saw her knife. She gripped it tightly in a hand slick with sweat, clinging to the desperate hope that it might be of some use against Oldfield, despite how little Ann's magic had done for her.

She wanted to yell at the other two, to scream at them to keep running and not to stop until there was no more strength left in them. But her breath caught in her throat even before she could try to form words. A knot of horror choked her as she ran.

"Run," she gasped as she reached them.

"They're not coming." Damon pointed back across the field.

"They will." Ines slid the knife away and grabbed them both by the arms. "Now run."

They dashed out of the park and down the street. The siren of a police car wailed as it shot past, strobing blue lights making their shadows dance.

"Could the police help?" Toby asked as they reached the end of the street.

"I don't think so." Damon pointed across the main road they had reached. Smoke billowed from the windows of an electronics shop, the twisted silhouettes of demons dancing in the blaze that lit its upper windows. Outside were dozens of young men and women, scarves across their faces and lengths of wood or pipe clutched in many of their hands. A dozen policemen were trying to quell the surging mob, while firefighters stood back, unable to get close to the blaze. A lone police officer stood by a patrol car on the near side of the street, screaming into his radio about a lack of backup. Another demon hovered above his head, insectile wings beating as it watched his expression grow fierce with fury.

"We should get out of here." Ines looked up and down the street, trying to work out which way was safest. Left would carry them back toward Ann Magrs's street, while right would take them straight past the angry mob.

A shooting star blazed through the sky, growing larger as it approached them, its light filling the darkened street. It stopped abruptly above the crowd, who stared up at it with bewilderment.

Rumiel had arrived.

Wings flapping majestically behind him, he raised a blazing sword above his head.

"Mortals," he cried out, "the judgement of the Lord has come. Fear not, for the Blazing Host will set your world to order and make right what has become corrupted."

"Crap." Without intending to, Ines felt herself drawing back into the shadows behind the police car, trying to make herself smaller, to recede into invisibility. Nausea still gripped her from the sight of Ann's bloody death. She was in no state for a confrontation.

"Get down." She yanked Toby down beside her, crouching in the deep shadows cast by the brightness of Rumiel's presence. Damon sank into the darkness. He thrust the papers into his pocket and pulled out his gold watch then put that away too with a shake of his head.

Rumiel began a speech about the glory of God and the fates of sinners, while Ines scrutinized the street, looking for a way to get past without being seen. There were front gardens here, but they were small spaces to hold dustbins and show off flower beds, not big enough for children to play in or to present much in the way of concealment. Just looking at how close the terraces loomed over them made her feel as if her world were closing in.

At least most of the gardens had some sort of wall or hedge, even if it was only a foot tall. Between those and the wheelie bins people kept out front, there was cover most of the way. They'd have to hop walls or scramble through hedges to get from garden to garden, and there would be quick dashes past open gateways, but if they timed it right, Rumiel might never see them.

It was better than nothing.

"Head for that garden." She pointed to one on the corner, its ground overshadowed by a bulky conifer. "We'll work our way down the street from there."

Rumiel was still occupied berating the crowd, but there was a streetlight on the corner they were heading for, and that would make it harder to stay hidden. Scrabbling in the gutter, Ines found an empty glass bottle. She took a moment to aim and then flung it at the light. There was a shower of shattering glass, and the pavement grew a little darker.

No one else paid it any attention, too preoccupied with the confrontation between the bellowing angel and the restless mass of humanity.

"Now." Ines sprinted across the road and into the shelter of the tree. Behind her came Damon, his low crouch particularly absurd given the length of his arms and legs.

Toby hadn't moved. He was staring straight into the blazing angelic light.

"Toby," Ines hissed.

He looked at her, frowned, and shook his head.

"Toby, come with me." She ran back to the car and grabbed him by the arm. "It's not safe out here."

"I can look after myself." He wriggled out of her grasp.

"Don't be an idiot. You're only twelve years old. How can you look after yourself?"

"Ways you can't." He glared at her. "I've got magic. And I'm sick of people bossing me around."

He tried to stand upright, his fist clenched around something, but Ines grabbed him and flung him over her shoulder. There was no time for this. She had to get them somewhere safe.

As she set off toward Damon, Toby twisted and tumbled from her grip. Before she could snatch him up, he was running from her, fist outstretched, mumbling the words of a spell. A green glow emerged from between his clenched fingers as he headed straight toward Rumiel.

"Oy!" he shouted. "You, angel!"

Rumiel turned, his smile like sunlight, the sword still above his head. His expression was the rigid smile of someone fighting to hold their temper in check. Flames flickered in his eyes.

"I know you," he intoned. "You are the brother of Ines Salgado."

His gaze fell upon Ines as she ran up behind Toby. The sight of the angel made her heart skip, and she stood frozen as emotions warred within her. Longing, compassion, rage, bitterness—a heady brew.

"You think you're so tough?" Toby opened his fist. "I'll show you."

Between his thumb and forefinger, he held a ball the size of a marble. It was black as the pit and yet glowed with a sickly green light. Something dripped from it and fell sizzling on the pavement.

"You side with the forces of Hell, Daniel Salgado?" Rumiel brought the sword around in front of him.

"I side with not you, arse face." Toby twitched the fingers of his other hand. Strands of the green glow curled around them.

Hope rose in Ines. Had she underestimated her brother? Could his ability with magic defend them? He was only twelve, but maybe he was special in a way she could never be. Maybe he—

Toby screamed. Something black was oozing from the ball, running from his hand down his wrist, clinging like tar to his arm. He waved his hand around, trying to shake it off, but the ball was stuck to him. His other hand, still tangled in the threads of magic, flailed through the air.

"You see this?" Rumiel pointed his sword at Toby, but he turned his face to the crowd. "This is what happens to those who align themselves with the powers of Hell. Theirs are the ways of sin, of misery, of chaos. Only by accepting the ways of Heaven, by embracing the order we bring, can you be safe."

"Screw you, pretty boy," someone yelled.

A bottle flew out of the crowd. With a flick of his wrist, Rumiel brought his sword around, easily blocking the missile. It exploded against his blade, spraying the angel with lager.

"Glowing wanker!" A brick followed the bottle, then stones and a corner of a paving slab. If the blows hurt Rumiel, it didn't show, but fury grew in his eyes.

"I bring you order!" he screamed. "That is all I do. All I have tried to do. Will none of you listen?"

Wings beating hard, he rose above the crowd, sword raised high.

"Listen, damn you!" His voice grew so loud, it made Ines's ears hurt. "Listen and obey!"

The crowd cowered before him, and for a moment, Ines thought Rumiel had won.

It was only for a moment.

"Screw you!" a woman screamed from the back of the crowd then turned and ran. The mob scattered as Rumiel swooped down upon them, swinging wildly with his sword.

"Listen!" he screamed, gliding down the road after the woman.

People ran screaming past Ines, policemen swiping at them with batons as demons emerged from the shadows left by Rumiel's departure. She ignored them all.

"Come on." She scooped Toby up in her arms. He was cold, his breath irregular, his face screwed up in pain.

"Here!" Damon stood by an abandoned police car, holding the rear door open.

"You know how to drive?" Still clutching Toby, Ines scrambled into the backseat.

"No, I thought we'd just sit here and wait to be arrested." Damon slammed the door shut behind her and slid into the driver's seat. He revved the engine and hit a switch on the dashboard. Blue lights started spinning above their heads. "Always wanted to do that."

The engine growled, and they jerked into motion, back up the street that had brought them there, past the park and on into the night.

"Better strap in," Damon said. "I've never done this before."

"You said you could drive!"

"No, I didn't."

They reached a roundabout, other cars stopping as they saw the blue lights. Trying to turn into the curve, Damon lost control. The car skidded across the road, across the roundabout, and hit another car with a crunch. The back window shattered, showering glass across the back of Ines's head.

"Come on!" Damon was out already and holding the door open.

People shouted and pointed as they ran from the car, across a petrol station forecourt, and down a back alley between residential streets. Ines paid them no attention. All she was aware of was the burden in her arms, a cold weight as motionless as a sack of sand. As the voices receded, she stopped, laid her brother on the ground, and knelt beside him. Her whole body trembled in fear as she placed her ear beside his mouth and listened.

"Oh God." Terror filled her veins with ice. "Damon, he's not breathing. I think Toby's dead."

CHAPTER 10
Risk of Loss

It was dark in the alley. There were no street lamps here. No stars or moon shone down from the cloudy sky. Thin shafts of light fell from around the curtains and blinds in the back rooms of the surrounding houses, but these bright lines only served to heighten the darkness in which they crouched.

"Toby." Ines shook her brother, desperate to see him stir. "Please, Toby, be alive."

Tears running down her cheeks, she pressed her mouth against his and breathed into him then moved her hands to pump at his chest. One of the summer camps their parents had sent her on taught CPR, but that had just been reviving a rubber doll. Never in her bleakest nightmares had she imagined using it on her kid brother.

"Breathe." She blew into his mouth again. "Come on, breathe."

"He's cold." Damon crouched next to her, his hand on Toby's arm.

"That could mean anything." Ines could feel the battle within her, a struggle between hope and loss. Even to her, she sounded desperate. "It doesn't have to mean he's dead."

She pumped at his chest, her movements growing ever more intense.

"No, it really doesn't." Something in Damon's voice sounded completely out of place, bright with realization. "Get back, Ines."

"No, I have to keep going." She blew into Toby's mouth again. "I have to!"

"No, you don't." Damon shoved her aside. In the shocked moment before she could respond, there was a flash of green light, and then Damon slumped back.

"What have you done?" Ines grabbed at her brother. "What have you—"

Toby groaned.

"Where am I?" he mumbled.

Laughing with relief, Ines flung her arms around him.

"Safe," she exclaimed. "I promise, you're safe."

* * *

"This is how it goes with my father's power." Damon sat on the edge of the bed, his face ashen. Just visible through the bathroom door, the ball of demonic power sat on the side of the sink, starkly black against the white porcelain. It was oozing again, and if there had been a deposit on the room, they would have lost it. As it was, the woman running the bed and breakfast had been happy just to take payment up front. There weren't so many guests in a city falling apart at the seams.

"What do you mean, this is how it goes?" Ines gestured at the other bed, where Toby had fallen into an exhausted sleep. She pulled her legs up beneath her on the chair, shrinking into herself as she tried to control the frustration bubbling within her. She didn't have many friends right now. She couldn't afford to lose the one she had by letting her anger get the most of her, but she couldn't say nothing and still stay sane. "You left it out for him to pick up!"

"I thought I'd just left it behind." Damon tried to run his gold watch across the back of his fingers but fumbled the movements. It fell to the floor, and he sat staring at his hand. "Idiot that I was, I thought I could do that. Just say no and forget about it."

"Anyone could have picked it up." Her hands tightened on the arms of the seat. "A little kid, an old lady, anyone."

"No, they couldn't." Damon looked as exhausted as she felt. "Remember, most people don't even see the magic all around them, not unless it's really in their faces. Only someone who was with me when the magic was offered, or who was part of our world, could have taken it. The way I saw it, worst-case scenario, Shaw takes away that little pool of temptation and uses it for something stupid. But as magical stupid is the Ministry's forte anyway, what difference would that make?"

"What difference would...?" There was a crack as a chair arm gave way beneath the pressure of Ines's wrath. "Listen to yourself, Damon. Just listen."

For a moment, there was fierceness in his eyes, and she was sure he would fight back. But then he hung his head, and his whole body slumped with shame.

"I should have thought about it more," he said. "It never occurred to me that"— he waved toward Toby—"that he would think to take it, never mind find a way to start unlocking the power. That was there for me, not him. I wanted to protect you both from it."

The wretchedness in his voice softened Ines's heart. It wasn't as if he'd ever meant to hurt her. She knew full well that she could count on Damon, as he'd proved over and again. If his father wanted to play games, to draw Damon into his monstrous world, that wasn't his fault.

There were no more words to share in anger. Instead, she rose, picked up the small kettle that sat on the chest of drawers, and filled it at the sink. Setting it to boil, she tipped a sachet of instant coffee into the bottom of a mug, and went to sit beside Damon.

Her pulse had just about reached a steady resting pace.

"I know it's not your fault." She turned the cup in her hands, looking at the little brown coffee specks tumbling over each other, powerless as their world shifted around them. "I just worry about Toby. I have to look after him."

"I know."

"And I know you saved him in the end."

"Saved him from winding up blackened and bruised from your CPR." The corner of his mouth twitched.

"His heart had stopped beating!" The outrage in her tone was mostly mocking. It was a relief to look back on how bad things had seemed, and how they had worked out in the end.

"His time had stopped moving." Damon picked up the watch. "Completely different."

"To a demon, maybe." Ines stood. The kettle had boiled. She poured steaming water into the mug and stirred it until the coffee dissolved. "But you know how you look to us mere mortals."

When she turned back to face him, Damon was stood by the sink, the black ball in his hand. His expression was intense, as if just holding the tiny thing were taking all of his willpower.

"It can't stick to you now, can it?" she asked. "Like it stuck to Toby?"

"No." With a heavy sigh, Damon slid the object into his pocket. "Its power is like my power—all about time. I can control it, channel it, absorb it." He took the proffered mug of coffee and returned to sitting on the bed. "Absorbing it would be the easiest thing, of course. That's what my father intends. One moment of acceptance, and all that power will go straight into me. I just might not be who I was anymore."

"Then don't do that." Ines sat back down and leaned her head on Damon's shoulder. "I like who you are."

"Me too." He wrapped his arm around her. "So what now?"

"Now..." Ines closed her eyes. "I don't know. I'm too tired to think straight. The important thing is, I need to look after Toby, to do what's best for him. Mum and Dad might need help, but I know he does.

I can't just boss him around—we've seen how that worked—but I can find ways to keep him safe."

"You're thinking leave him somewhere while we take on the Ministry?"

"Maybe. I'm not sure what's more dangerous—leaving him without protection, or taking him to dangerous places knowing that at least we'll be there for him."

"Whatever you choose, I'm sure it'll be right." Damon squeezed her tightly. "I believe in you, and so does Toby, even if he doesn't say it."

They sat in silence, Ines enjoying the feeling of Damon sitting next to her, the comfort of his arm around her. She could have been perfectly contented like this, if this were all there was to life. Just sitting with Damon, knowing they had each other, listening to him breathing. The smell of his coffee, something she herself found too bitter, was comfortingly part of him. If the world would let her, she could have sunk into this moment forever and never emerged.

She opened her eyes, and the world came crashing in. Toby, pale and still beneath the duvet of the other bed. The peeling wallpaper of a run-down bed and breakfast a hundred miles from home. The black stain on the ceiling that reminded her that there were demons out there in the world—real, malevolent demons, not a kindhearted half demon like Damon. Even the knife she had left by the door, ready in case of an emergency, was a reminder of the dangers in this world and of how they were changing her. Once this was over, once her family was safe and the world was something like normal, maybe then she could have the comfort she wanted. Not before.

Setting aside his empty mug, Damon turned to look at her. His face was only inches from hers, and she could feel herself sinking into the dark, soulful depths of his eyes. With one hand, she reached up, trying to assert order upon black hair left dishevelled by a day on the run. But she could assert no order there and wasn't sure she wanted to. There was something endearing about the wildness of his look.

"Damon," she began, "we should—"

That was as far as she got. He leaned in, his lips against hers, and she lost herself in the kiss. It was wild and passionate, all Damon's calm and restraint cast away. She abandoned restraint too, throwing herself into the longing for him. They clung tightly to each other, and for a long, glorious moment, she dreamed of never letting go.

But the world had its claws in her.

She drew back, disentangling herself. Looking up into his smile, she felt dread at the thought that she might break that look forever. But what choice did she have?

"Damon," she whispered. "You know that I want to be with you."

His smile widened.

"I want to be with you too." He leaned in to kiss her again, but she backed away. As she stood, stuffing her hands into the pockets of her hoodie, he looked up in confusion. "What is it, Ines?"

"I can't," she said. "Not this. Not now."

"What?" He jerked to his feet. "Why? That makes no sense! The world's going to hell, and you want to throw away what's good in it?"

"I don't want to throw it away." She couldn't stand to look at him. Instead, she went to the window, twitching back the faded blue curtain to look out onto the night-shrouded street below. "But I can't afford to throw away what we have. Our friendship, it's the only thing that's kept me going through the last month. All the violence, the chaos, the danger. Losing my parents. Nearly losing Toby just now. I can't afford to risk losing you."

"You won't lose me." Damon laughed. "You just get a side of me you wouldn't otherwise."

Ines shook her head.

"I've seen relationships," she said. "They don't last. Especially not at our age." The words made her feel weary and beaten down, old before her time. "I can't lose what I have with you now. You're this perfect still space in my life. You keep me going when the whole world falls apart."

Silence filled the room. It weighed upon her like a mountain of sorrow.

"Please say something," she said at last.

"Okay." Taking a deep breath, Damon got to his feet. He walked over to stand beside her. "I understand. It makes sense. Whatever you need from me, however you need it, I'm here for you. And if that means waiting for something more, I can live with that."

He put his arm around her again, and she wrapped hers around him, pulling him close.

"Thank you," she whispered into his chest. "Thank you so much."

"That's okay," he said.

But there was a dead weight in his voice.

CHAPTER 11
Siding With Humanity

Ines hunkered down over her breakfast, trying to ignore the argument coming from the kitchen of the bed and breakfast. At least the staff had served them before they lost their tempers. The toast might be burnt and the sausages undercooked, but she desperately needed the energy. She felt as if she'd run a marathon the day before, and had another one ahead of her today.

"Do you think there's a demon in with them?" Toby whispered, peering past her toward the kitchen door.

"Probably." Ines focused on her mug of tea. Perverse as the thought was, demons were the least of their problems.

If an angel turned up, or anyone in a gray suit, then she'd start worrying.

There was a crash of breaking crockery. The only other guest still in the dining room got up from her seat and hurried away.

"You think you can run this place without me?" someone yelled. "Fine! Just you bloody try."

A door slammed, and silence descended. A moment later, somebody started to sob.

The sound tugged at Ines. She stiffened, her instincts telling her to get up and comfort whoever was in the kitchen. But a glance at Toby reminded her of why she hadn't gotten involved while the argument was still raging. His skin was pale, eyes darting nervously around. Anything that risked bringing more trouble into his life was something she wasn't going near.

She stuffed a forkful of bacon and eggs into her mouth and kept her eyes focused on the plate. At the edge of her vision, another plate sat across the table, its contents growing cold. Damon had run off, phone in hand, before their breakfast even arrived. However often she told herself that he would come back, after the previous night's conversation, she felt the nagging of doubt.

What if they couldn't still be friends, given how he felt about her? Had she ruined everything by giving in to the temptation of that kiss?

A man in a grease-stained apron emerged from the kitchen. His face was blotchy, and he rubbed a hand across his eyes. As he looked up and saw them, he froze.

"I could..." Even those two words sounded choked up. Shoulders slumping, he walked out of the room without another word. As he passed them, they saw a black figure clinging to his back, like a tiny monkey with horns and a barbed tail. It shot out a long red tongue, licking beads of sweat from the back of the cook's neck.

Ines tightened her grip on her knife, just in case, but the demon ignored them.

Breakfast tasted like ashes in her mouth, but it was better than going hungry.

Footsteps made her cling tighter to the knife. Tensed and ready, she watched to see who would come in this time.

Damon appeared, his black shirt rumpled, eyes on the phone he held in front of him. He didn't look up until he was at the table.

"Mum says hi." He put away the phone and set to tackling his breakfast. "Actually, she says she's glad I'm helping you, and she hopes we're all alright, and if there's anything she can do, we just have to ask." He forced a grin. "Nice to be reminded that only one of my parents is an arsehole."

"Is she alright?" Ines asked. He looked worried, and that worried her. "The Ministry haven't tried to get to you through her, have they?"

He swallowed a mouthful of toast and washed it down with a gulp of coffee before replying.

"She's safe." This time, his grin was tainted with bitterness. "Well, as safe as anyone can be now."

Setting down his knife and fork, he pulled out his phone and slid it across the table. It was open to the front page of the BBC News website.

"Riot In Trafalgar Square," the headline read. "PM Promises Prompt Action."

There were pictures with the article. Barricades of overturned cars and broken benches. Lines of riot police, their plastic shields forming a wall beneath Nelson's Column. The flaming tail of a Molotov cocktail as it twisted through the air, its moment against the night sky immortalized by a photographer's perfect timing.

"But London was supposed to be safe!" Ines stared at the images. "After what we did..."

"What did we do?" Damon pushed aside his plate. "Got lucky mostly. The barrier was already damaged by the time we got involved. Stopping Oldfield caused some kind of backlash, and that kept the city safe for a while. But even if we've kept out the supernatural influences, that can only do so much.

"Think about it. All the people in the country affected by demons and angels, they don't know what's going on. All they know is that they feel furious, or desperate, or ecstatic, or whatever's being exaggerated in their minds. They'll focus those feelings on what they care about already, whether it's binge drinking or protesting against the government. A lot of those people have reasons to go into London, and just because the demons and angels can't follow them there, that doesn't mean that they won't still be feeling what they felt. That would be like expecting an abuse victim to feel fine the moment they get away from their attacker."

He had his watch in his hand, turning it around and around between two fingers and a thumb. Through the dining room doors, in the lobby of the bed and breakfast, a clock struck nine.

"It's about more than London, isn't it?" Ines said. "The longer the barrier's broken, the harder it'll get to undo the harm. This could destroy people's lives."

"Could?" Damon looked at her with a terrible intensity. "It already has. The only question is, how many more will be lost."

"Can we fix it?" Toby's voice trembled with fear.

That soft, broken tone almost brought Ines to tears. Wrapping her arms around her brother, she pulled him close.

"We will fix it," she said. "I promise."

"How?" he asked, and she could see the same question in Damon's raised eyebrows.

"I don't know." Ines clung tightly to her brother. "What I do know is that it has to be done, and no one else is going to do it. The angels are enjoying setting the world to what they consider to be right. The demons are gorging themselves on the worst of human behaviour. Even the Ministry, the people who should be protecting us, are trying to leach off the barrier's power, despite the cost."

Damon took a deep breath, his face grim.

"You're right." He downed the dregs of his coffee. "Someone has to stand up. Looks like it's going to be us."

A door banged open, and a gust of wind swept in through the lobby. At the sound of heavy footsteps, Ines rose, table knife still in hand. Damon wasn't much of a fighter, but he was on his feet too.

A bell rang in reception.

"Yo, service!" a man shouted. "Isn't anyone here?"

Tension eased from Ines's muscles. She exchanged a look of relief with Damon.

"Just another customer," he said.

"We should get going anyway." She pulled her bag from under the table. "You ready?"

"Always." Damon patted his satchel. "That almost sounded manly, didn't it?"

"Almost." She smiled.

"Where are we going?" Toby asked.

"Coffee shop," she replied. "That's where Damon gets all his best ideas."

"All my ideas are best."

"You guys are being weird." Toby shook his head and led the way out of the room. As he walked into the lobby, his face fell.

A moment later, Ines saw why.

The lobby of the bed and breakfast had the same run-down vibe as the rest of the place. The brown-and-green paint scheme, which might have been fashionable decades before, looked faded as well as vile. The carpet was worn thin, a rug covering the worst of it by the reception desk.

In front of that desk stood the only thing in the room that wasn't grubby or worn. Shining brightly through his white tracksuit, the bell from the counter clutched in his hand, the angel Sanctus smiled triumphantly at them.

"At last." He flung the bell over his shoulder. It hit a mirror, which shattered and fell in gleaming shards. "I knew I'd find you if I just kept looking."

Cracking his knuckles, he approached them with a boxer's slow sway, the light of his presence reflected in fractured fragments from the broken mirror and the dusty plastic chandelier that hung above their heads.

"We don't want any trouble." Ines drew her knife. She'd dealt with Sanctus before, though then she'd been fighting on Rumiel's side.

"Oh, but I do." Sanctus raised his fists. "Michael wants you brought in, but only Rumiel wants you unharmed. And there's a lot of us looking to balance the scales of justice after what happened at Oldfield's."

"I suppose we've all got things we want revenge for." Thinking of the misery the angels had put her through, she waved the knife in front of her. She had no qualms about stabbing supernatural creatures. "Toby, take my bag and head out the door. Damon, you go with him."

"We can—"

"Just go."

She leapt.

The cruelty had been obvious in Sanctus's eyes. Even as she suggested that her companions get clear, he was leaning toward the door, getting ready to block their escape. That gave her an opening.

Fast as she was, Sanctus was faster. Twisting away from the knife thrust, he swung a punch at her face. She ducked, rolled, and came up next to the counter, raising the knife between them again.

"You're good." Sanctus ignored Toby and Damon as they headed out the door. "Shame you've chosen to side with evil."

"The only side I've chosen is humanity."

Ines leapt onto the reception desk, dodging a kick that splintered its front.

Swinging her blade in a series of swift slashes, she forced Sanctus to back up. As he stooped into a defensive stance, she jumped, grabbing the grubby chandelier with one hand and kicking him in passing as she swung across the room. She felt the jolt as her feet hit his head, then fingers closing like a steel clamp around her ankle.

Sanctus yanked on Ines's leg, slamming her into the floor. Pain hit her in a dozen places, and she tasted blood, but that wasn't going to slow her down. She twisted onto her back, slamming her free heel into his wrist as she did so. He let go but leapt on top of her, pinning her to the ground.

"This is what you get for defying us." His fist slammed into her face, then her chest, then her stomach. It was like a hammer pounding at her flesh, turning her body into a mass of pain. "There will be order. There will be law. His word will be done."

Gasping with pain, Ines felt her fingers loosening on the knife. She tried to kick, tried to twist, tried to free herself any way she could, but he kept her pressed down, trapped beneath the weight of muscle.

Tightening her grip on the knife, she channeled all her strength into a single movement and slammed the blade into Sanctus's side. He grunted, and the knife jammed against his ribs, but she kept pushing, driving it deeper into him. His fingers grabbed her arm, forcing it back. With the last of her strength, she twisted her wrist. The knife scraped against whatever was inside the angel. He let out a scream of pain and fell away from her, grabbing at the weapon protruding from him.

Ines didn't stop to see what damage she had done. She was on her feet and out the door, racing into the street.

"Run!" she yelled at Damon and Toby, who stood waiting on the pavement. "Run like your lives depend on it."

CHAPTER 12
The Wayfarer's Rest

Years of exercise and martial arts training had given Ines speed and endurance out of proportion to her small frame. On her own, she could outrun almost anyone she knew.

When the people she knew needed to keep up, that became a problem.

Damon grimaced and clutched his side as they rounded the corner. He wasn't panting as badly as Toby, but neither of them looked fit to run for long. Knowing that Sanctus might be coming, it was all Ines could do to slow to their pace. She'd never been more frustrated.

"Just keep going," she shouted.

Glancing back, she saw no sign of the angel following them. That didn't mean much. She scanned the skies and listened for the beating of wings, certain that he would descend on them at any moment.

Unless she really had done him some harm. Was that possible? The satisfaction that followed the thought was followed by a moment of nausea. What was she becoming, that she could take pleasure in stabbing someone, even someone who wanted her dead?

The tip of her tongue stung where she had bitten it during the fight. She spat a mouthful of blood out on the pavement.

"Here, what's going on?" A woman stood in her front garden, newspaper in hand, staring at them as they ran past. "What happened to you kids?"

They kept running.

Ines's thoughts changed gear. In the desperate moment of flight, she hadn't considered what they would look like to the people they passed. But not everyone was caught up in a supernatural war, and three frantically running teenagers would draw attention at the best of times. With riots in the streets, and Ines's face swollen with bruises, they would be lucky to go a mile without being stopped by the authorities. Then what? How would she explain the bruises, their presence in Manchester, the knives in her bag?

Picking up the pace, she overtook the others. They'd followed her this far—maybe she could lead them to some sort of safety.

A closed-down pub sat on a corner of the next street, graffiti scrawled across the boards blocking its windows and doors. A sign swung in the breeze outside, its rusty chain squealing. Beneath a picture of an old roadside inn was written the name Wayfarer's Rest.

After everything she'd been through, Ines didn't know whether to believe in omens. What she did believe in was abandoned buildings.

She ducked down the side of the pub, past a pile of crumbling wooden pallets. Stopping at a side door, she looked around in case anyone was watching. The only people in sight were Damon and Toby, red faced and sweating as they ran after her.

The lock on the door had been neglected long enough to get rusty, but that didn't make it any less sturdy. The boards covering the window next to it, on the other hand, had started to warp with age. She wormed her fingers in behind the loosest-looking one and heaved. Her muscles ached from the fight, but necessity lent her a strength she had thought exhausted. Nails popped free, wood splintered, and the board came away in her hand.

It was a moment's work to pull the next board free then use it to smash the glass from the window. While the others caught their breath, Ines clambered through the gap.

As her eyes adjusted to the dark, she saw that she was in a near-empty storage room. There were a few cardboard boxes gathering dust on a high shelf and a cluster of metal beer barrels in a corner, presumably empty. An open door led onto a corridor.

It would do.

She slid back the bolt on the outer door and wrestled with the rusty latch until it finally gave way. The door swung open, and she ushered Damon and Toby inside.

"Should we be in here?" Toby asked, looking nervously around. "This is trespassing."

"The police have higher priorities right now than checking on empty business-es." Ines glanced once more at the sky outside then closed the door. If Sanctus was following them, then he was being subtle about it, and that didn't seem like his style.

The pub's main taproom was as dusty and empty as the storage room but otherwise in surprisingly good condition. Cushioned stools sat around the tables, and empty glasses were lined up behind the bar. Everything had been tidied up before the place was shut down. Perhaps the owner had been expecting to reopen, or maybe he took pride in what he was leaving behind for the next landlord—a landlord who had never come.

A flick of a switch proved that the electricity was still on, lights revealing a green carpet and matching upholstery, as well as a mirror behind the bar. Damon pulled out a table next to an ornamental fireplace and sank into the seat behind it.

"What now?" There was an old clock in a gilt frame on the mantelpiece. He took it down and started winding the mechanism.

"Rest. Hide." Ines sat opposite him, took off her hoodie, and examined her bruises. Large parts of her body ached, and she was sure it would get worse as the adrenaline wore off. "We can't fight the angels—they're just too strong. So whatever else we do, we need to stay hidden from them."

"I agree." Damon took out his watch then turned the hands of the clock until they told the right time. "And I have an idea to help us with that."

"What sort of idea?"

"Magic." He set the clock down in the middle of the table. It ticked softly and steadily.

"You didn't want to use your power." Ines took her friend's hand. "Don't do this if it's going to hurt you."

Damon squeezed her hand and then let go. Picking up the clock, he walked to the center of the room and set it down on the floor.

"I'm not going to tap into what my father tried to give me." Going behind the bar, he rummaged around on shelves and in cupboards, doors thudding open and bottles clinking as he moved them aside. "Just a portion of what I had before."

"And the need for suffering to power it?"

Damon gave her a wry grin. "I think we've got enough of that."

"If you think it's worth it." Ines realized she was too tired to stay upright on her stool, never mind to argue with Damon. A couple of steps took her to the cushioned seats against the wall, and she lay down gratefully, letting her battered muscles rest.

With a saltcellar in his hand, Damon walked in a circle around the clock, leaving a trail of white grains behind him. His movements were meticulously smooth, forming a perfect ring on the carpet.

"Can I help?" Toby sounded half nervous, half eager.

"Have you ever done a preparatory cleansing?" Damon set aside the salt and looked at the younger boy.

It seemed easiest not to get involved. Ines doubted that Toby could contribute to whatever Damon had planned, and even if he could, Damon would find a way to put him off.

"Totally." Toby held his hands up, fingers at odd angles. "You start like this, and then you—"

"Cool." Damon cut him short. "Looks like you know what you're doing, so can you clear the area while I build the ward?"

"Totally!"

"I'm not sure about this." Ines propped herself up on one elbow.

"It'll be fine." Damon came close and lowered his voice to a whisper. "I know you want to protect him, but part of that is letting him learn to protect himself. I'll be doing all the tricky stuff this time."

Reluctantly, Ines nodded her head.

"OK, but be careful," she said. "What are you doing, anyway?"

"I'll be interfering with the transit of supernatural phenomena through time, in a limited area around us." Damon raised his voice so that Toby could hear too. "It should make it harder for our enemies to find us—angels, demons, and mages, they all rely on magic for surveillance. I think it could also help with the Barrier of Mercy.

"In a very real sense, the Barrier is around us all the time. If I can stall changes in magic, then that will slow down the Barrier's disintegration and could even be used to fix it—effectively reversing time to make repairs. For now, it'll just be local, but if it works, then we're one step closer to a lasting solution.

"You want to fix the Barrier? This is how we start."

"You're amazing sometimes." Ines smiled. Damon had never seemed like more of a hero—calm, confident, and in control of his power. It was all she could do to resist reaching out and kissing him, but she had made her decision. She had to be strong.

"Just not the amazing you want right now, huh?" Damon frowned. Then he was in action again, heading back to the clock in the middle of the room. "I'd better save the world so that we can get on with our lives." He looked back at Ines. "All the parts of our lives."

She smiled and sank onto the cushions, watching her two favorite boys in action.

Under Damon's guidance, Toby helped to put together the parts of the spell. Lacking any gift for magic herself, Ines couldn't see half of what they were doing, never mind understand what it meant. But as she watched her brother's growing pleasure at being able to take part, as she saw his confidence rise and the color return to his face, she was more grateful than ever for having Damon in her life.

Jealousy added a dark tinge to her thoughts. Wonderful as it was to watch them working together, it made her intensely aware of how much she was left out of the world of magic, the one occupied by her family and her closest friend. There were connections here, opportunities to work together that she would never have. She would never cast a spell with Damon, as Toby was doing now, their power intertwining as glowing strands above the steadily ticking clock. She would never be able to fully participate in conversations about this side of their lives or to understand everything it meant to them.

That thought was one more source of weariness, on top of lost sleep and the battering she had received from Sanctus. Her eyelids drooped, and her mind wandered, thoughts drifting in the disconnected haze on the verge of dreams. The ticking of the clock grew slower, lulling her toward sleep.

A shout woke her with a start. She bolted upright, fists raised.

"No, no, no!" Damon clutched the clock in his hands. The circle of salt glowed around him, casting a red light across his face. Toby was watching him with alarm, hands raised, a blue glow between them.

The clock ticked at an ever-accelerating speed, going faster and faster until the individual sounds blurred together in an insectile buzz.

"Shut it down," Damon called out.

Toby sank to his knees, placing his hands on the circle. As the blue and red glows met, they merged and then vanished in a brief flash of white light.

With a tinkle of flying parts, the back of the clock exploded, spraying gears across the floor.

"Damn it." Damon flung the clock away, its glass front smashing against the wall. He sank to his knees then looked up at Toby. "It's spreading, isn't it?"

There was a moment of quiet as Toby closed his eyes and stretched his arms out to either side, fingers twitching in the air. When he opened his eyes again, his expression was downcast.

He nodded.

"Shit." Damon smacked his fist against the floor. "I wasn't strong enough, not with the power I have."

"So it didn't work." Ines placed a hand on his shoulder. "We'll find other ways to hide."

"The chaos from the breaking of the Barrier, it hooked into the spell." Damon looked up, crestfallen. "Instead of slowing it down, I've sped up the disintegration. I tried to save us, and instead, I've made things far worse."

CHAPTER 13
Out of Hell

Finding a working radio behind the bar didn't change anything that mattered. It didn't tell them anything about where Ines's parents were. It didn't drive back the demons or hide them from the angels. It didn't slow down the disintegration of the barrier. But it did at least provide something like entertainment, a break from focusing on the misery of their situation.

The local radio station had reverted to emergency playlists so that it could keep going without DJs braving the streets of a country going mad. The songs had clearly been chosen a decade ago, and by someone whose tastes were outdated even then. Cheesy riffs and orchestral strings accompanied an ageing rocker bellowing about what he would and wouldn't do for love.

"At least it's not Phil Collins." Damon lay on the bar, looking blankly at the ceiling.

"Phil who?" Toby asked.

"Oh, the sweet innocence of youth."

The song ended, and a rambling guitar introduction began.

"Bat out of Hell," Damon said. "How wretchedly fitting."

At a table in the corner of the room, Ines looked again at her supplies. Three knives, all of which she'd sharpened to a deadly edge. A couple of changes of underwear. Tampons. Enough junk food to get them through another day, two if they were careful with it.

Restraint in eating seemed unlikely. Running and fighting were exhausting, and they all needed the extra carbs. Even if they didn't, avoiding comfort eating was an act of willpower, and they were all too emotionally drained to spare that energy.

"If we're going to stay here, then we'll need to go get supplies," she said.

"Agreed." Damon was staring intently at something in his hand. "But before we do that, I—wait, what's happening?"

The music had fallen abruptly silent, replaced by a ticking sound, a moment of static, and then the well-spoken voice of an announcer.

"The following is a message from the prime minister," he said.

Another voice emerged, even posher than the last one.

"People of Britain," the prime minister began, "as you are aware, the past week has seen a sudden increase in lawlessness and violence. In times of crisis, it is the duty of government to look to the security both of our great nation and of you, its people. To this end, and with the full support of both Parliament and Her Majesty the Queen, I have declared a state of emergency. Armed forces are being deployed to help the police maintain law and order. The first troops are already on the ground in many major cities, but wherever you are, whatever your circumstances, be assured—help is on its way.

"You can also take steps to ensure your own safety. Please stay indoors. If there is a medical emergency, then call 999, and emergency services will come to you. Workers in high-priority professions will be contacted with instructions for safe travel to and from work. Until you receive such a call, please remain at home.

"The police and the army have orders to restrain anyone found at large without the appropriate permits. Stay safe, stay at home, and be assured—help is on its way.

"Together, we can weather this storm."

There was more clicking, and then the music returned.

Scenes from London replayed in Ines's memory. Soldiers and policemen, as vulnerable to supernatural influence as anyone else, giving way to the violent urges that demons provoked. Men with guns wouldn't make the streets any safer. They just ensured the violence would be deadly.

"Why don't they understand?" Toby asked. "They've got a whole Ministry for this stuff."

"Oldfield is the minister now." Just saying the name brought forth Ines's bitterness and rage. "She's got the

Ministry too busy with her plans to help the government out."

"Or maybe she's lying to them to further her plans." Damon sat up, a determined expression on his face. "Either way, it's down to us to save the day. Much as I hate to sound like some musclehead from a movie, it's time for extreme action."

He held out his hand. The tiny black orb of power sat in the middle of his palm, sucking up light so that his skin seemed to descend into a world of shadow.

"Don't." Ines got to her feet. "There are other ways to do this."

"To do what?" Damon asked. "We can't even work out our next step with the resources we have. I need to start using my power, and I need as much of it as I can muster."

"You wanted to avoid your father's influence, and now you're giving in to it. Think of what it could do to you."

"I am. But I'm also thinking about what could happen to the people I love if things keep going like this." He closed his hand around the orb. "I'm doing this for Mum and for you."

"You can't do this for me."

"You'd do it for Toby. Let me try to live up to your example."

Ines looked at her brother. There was fear on his face as he stared at Damon's hand. Fear and grief had been his life for weeks now. She couldn't deny anything that might make him safer.

"Alright," she said. "Do it."

"I already am," Damon replied through gritted teeth.

The view of his hand grew hazy, as if it were seen through the hot air above a road in summer. His fingers tightened, turning white at the knuckles. In his other hand, he was holding his gold pocket watch, tapping the back with one finger as the seconds ticked by.

"This may... may take a while." Damon sank to his knees, sweat beading on his forehead. "I have to unlock it, channel it, absorb it, then... Urgh."

He curled up and lay on his side on the floor, his breath rasping, legs twitching. Shadows darkened at the corners of the room.

Helplessness consumed Ines. She knew no magic, had no way of even beginning to help. It was awful to feel useless in the face of her friend's suffering, worse yet to think that he was doing this for her. Desperate for something to do, she took off her hoodie and draped it over him then sat down, nestling his head in her lap.

"You can do this." She brushed back the hair sticking to his clammy forehead. "I believe in you."

"Such a touching sight." The demon Eldervain's voice was a mocking hiss. He seemed to have formed out of the shadows in one corner of the pub, hat pulled down low over his bulbous eyes. "Lord Chron will be delighted."

"What are you doing here?" Ines formed a fist with one hand, the other resting protectively on Damon.

"Can't an old demon take pleasure in seeing his work bear fruit?"

"He's in pain! How can you enjoy this?"

"When in Hell." The demon shrugged, his ill-fitting suit flapping around him.

"Get away from us." Ines glanced at the table with her knives on it, working out how quickly she could get from Damon to there and then to the demon. She'd killed the first of his kind she met, and she wasn't averse to doing it again.

"As you wish. But one last thing before I go. This disturbance has drawn the attention of others. You should be ready for trouble."

He backed into the corner he had come from, his suit merging with the shadows.

"What sort of attention?" Ines asked. "Come back, you dickhead. Tell me what I need to know."

But the demon was gone, vanished into darkness.

Bright light flashed through a gap in the boards over the windows.

"Angels." Ines looked down at Damon then up at the windows again. Had the angelic host really sensed what Damon was doing, or was this just coincidence? After all, Eldervain wouldn't want them to close the barrier any more than he would want Damon to resist his father's power. This was the work of a demon, a creature of danger and deceit.

Taking her hoodie from where she had draped it over Damon, she rolled it up into a ball. As pillows went it wouldn't be much worse than her legs, and it would free her up to act.

"Stay there." Toby was by the window, peering through the dirty glass and the gap in the boards beyond. "I've got an idea."

"Get away from there." Ines leapt to her feet. "You're twelve years old—you can't go fighting angels!"

"I'm nearly thirteen. And anyway, I'm not going to fight them." He twitched his fingers in a way she had only ever seen mages do. The air glowed around his hands. "I'm going to distract them."

"Toby, don't!"

It was too late. The magic shimmered and then scattered from around his hands. There was a shout from the street.

Rushing to the window, Ines peered outside. Two angels stood in the road, glowing with heavenly power. Their immaculate white suits and perfect faces made them look like something out of a dream, but the swords in their hands turned it into a nightmare, fire dancing along deadly blades.

Beyond them, a shadow was shifting in the entrance to a side street. A vaguely human shape, its edges blurred into the scenery around it, merging with brick walls and concrete paving slabs. It seemed to be creeping away from the angels.

"You think we cannot see you, abomination?" one of the angels exclaimed, pointing at the shape. "Your pitiful camouflage cannot hide you from the blades of the righteous."

Toby twisted his hands, and the shadow moved faster, its movements going from a slow stalk to a run as it raced away down the street and around a corner. The angels ran after it, one of them singing a song of blood and vengeance in a high, melodic voice. Then they too turned the corner and disappeared from view.

"Told you." Toby smiled at Ines. "If you're allowed to protect me, you've got to let me protect you sometimes. Just like you and Damon were talking about."

"That doesn't work when one of us is just a kid." Ines wrapped an arm around him. "Still, that was really well done."

Something about the situation still didn't feel quite right. But then, if she felt safe now, then there would be something wrong with her.

Stepping away from the window, she headed back toward Damon. As she knelt beside him, a bright line of light burst through the window.

Too late, she realized what had been wrong. The world outside the pub hadn't returned to normal daylight after the two angels left.

There was another one out there.

Time seemed to slow as she turned, frozen in the moment of decision between going for her knives and going for Toby. The decision was taken from her as the window exploded inward, splinters of wood and glass flying in a blaze of light like the heart of the sun. Toby tumbled backwards, and she screamed as blood ran from his face.

Sanctus stood in the frame of the broken window. There was nothing beautiful or glorious about his expression, only fury that bordered on the insane.

"Ines Salgado," he boomed. "I am going to mess you up so badly."

CHAPTER 14
The Blood of Angels

The room was filled with light, so bright it chased away the shadows everywhere except around Damon. For a moment, he seemed to stir, responding to Sanctus's arrival despite the internal struggle in which he was engaged. But it was only a shudder of movement before he sank back to the ground.

Ines barely noticed. She was horrified at the sight of Toby lying bleeding on the floor. Only the menace of Sanctus as he leapt into the room could distract her from the sight.

"You think you're so tough?" he said. "Think you're so smart, hiding in a darkened hole like a scared little mouse, playing with pitiful distractions?

I am going to destroy you, and then I'll destroy your little friends. The Kingdom of Heaven stops for no mortal."

"I don't know what Heaven's really like," Ines said. "But if you count as good there, then it can go to Hell."

She darted toward the knives, but Sanctus was ahead of her, blocking the way to the table. His knuckle-dusters shone as he whipped out with his fist, smacking Ines in the shoulder. She spun around, just managing to retain her balance, ducked a second punch, and shifted back, fists raised. Knives had never been a natural part of her fighting style anyway. She knew judo. She knew Krav Maga. She could take on this gleaming pillar of pomposity with his shining tracksuit and shinier eyes.

Sanctus prowled in a slow circle around her, shifting from foot to foot like a boxer warming up at the start of a match. He jabbed at her once, twice, three times, testing her defences. More cautious than she remembered. Less impulsive than she expected.

Running her gaze up and down his body, she looked for any sign of a misstep or badly planned move. It didn't seem likely that an angel would have a weak knee or a wonky hip, but there was one sign of hope. A slash showed in his tracksuit where she had stabbed him earlier, and the glimpse of flesh beneath it looked broken. Was he still recovering?

This time, his attack was for real, a swift series of blows that sent her back across the room as she dodged and wove, blocked and parried. He almost forced her into a corner, but at the last moment, she leapt left, vaulting a table and landing in the open. As he turned, she leapt to the center of the room, seizing the open ground, before going on the offensive.

The techniques she had learnt were more about defense than offense, but that didn't mean they couldn't be used in other ways. If nothing else, fighting for her life had taught her to fight dirty. She advanced on Sanctus with a series of kicks. As he swung a punch, she grabbed his arm, twisted, and lifted.

It wasn't a perfect throw, but it was as good as she could get against a man of his size. He was lifted from his feet, across her back, and through the air. She felt a moment of triumph, then of terrible acceptance as wings burst from his back and he halted in midair, hovering in front of the window, light shining out around him.

"Perhaps Rumiel's right," Sanctus said. "Perhaps you could have helped us build a better world, if you weren't so desperate to protect this broken one."

With a snap of his wings, he hurtled toward Ines.

At the very last moment, she dropped, not trying to break her own fall as she slammed into the ground. All her effort went into a single punch, straight up into his side as he swept over her. Fingers extended, she hit with all of her strength, the ground against her back giving her extra leverage. Her arm shuddered as she hit hard muscle, but she didn't flinch.

The blow was perfect, right on the spot where she had stabbed him before. There was resistance, but her fingers penetrated the wound, driving into the warmth of Sanctus's body. She curled her fingers around and dug in then jerked her arm, driving her fist deeper.

Sanctus screamed like a wild beast, twisting as he fell to the ground. Arms, legs, and wings thrashed as he tried desperately to throw her off. But the movements were uncoordinated, as wild as his screeching, the instinctive defense of an animal in pain, not the fighting style of a trained and experienced combatant.

Something oozed down Ines's arm, and her flesh burned inside the angel, but she kept hold. He was on top of her again, crushing her beneath his weight. She flexed her fingers, splayed them out, and then tightened them into a fist once more, Sanctus's screams rising with each movement.

At last, the pain became too much. She jerked back her arm.

Sanctus staggered to his feet. His hands clutched his side. He swung back his foot to kick Ines, who was now curled up in pain, clutching her injured arm close. She had almost defeated him, and now she could barely defend herself.

A beam of darkness shot across the room, hitting Sanctus in his injured side. The wound widened, fluid flowing from it like thick golden blood.

"Get away from her." Damon was on his knees, one hand holding him up, the other pointed at Sanctus. "Or I'll speed the bleeding up so much, you die right here, right now, without ever coming near your host again."

"You would not dare, demon." Sanctus's certainty wavered.

"Try me."

The two of them locked eyes for a long moment, then Sanctus staggered to the window, stretched his wings, and flapped limply away.

A fragment of glass fell from the frame and tinkled as it hit the floor.

"So much for hiding." Damon crawled over to Ines and helped her sit up. The pain was receding from her hand, the golden ooze of Sanctus's innards dripping onto the carpet. Moving the hand still hurt, but she could at least bring herself to flex her fingers again.

As the haze of pain faded from her brain, she remembered who else had been injured.

"Toby!" She scrambled across the litter of glass and wood to her brother's side. He was unconscious but still breathing. Blood ran from wounds on his face and hands, glass embedded in his flesh. But alarming as the wounds looked, they weren't bleeding heavily.

With Damon's help, she lifted Toby onto a table. They found plasters, gauze, and disinfectant in an old first aid kit on the wall of the men's room, and the taps were still connected. As Ines carefully extracted the shards of glass, Damon cleaned and covered the wounds.

"Ow!" Toby wriggled as she retrieved one of the longer pieces from his cheek. Unable to restrain herself, she flung her arms around him in relief.

"You're alive." She squeezed him tightly.

"I hurt," he whimpered.

It seemed such a ridiculously small way to describe his injuries, Ines couldn't help but laugh.

"What's so funny?" Toby said in bewilderment.

"Just... just... just being alive." She shook her head, unable to stop. Damon was laughing too, and then Toby. Maybe it was shock, or maybe it was the joy of survival, but for that moment, Ines was willing to just be happy.

Then a pair of wings flapped outside, and hands gripped the window frame.

Ines took a deep breath, closed her eyes, and mustered what strength she could. There was no way she could win another fight now. Her hand felt as if it had been set on fire. Her back was one massive bruise. Muscles she had thought in good shape were going stiff from the strains of the morning's fighting.

She turned to face the window.

"Whoever you are, I just beat the angel Sanctus half to death." She raised her fists and stepped in front of Toby. "I will gut you where you stand if you mess with us."

Even if she couldn't win, she was going to go down fighting and defiant to the end.

"I do not intend to mess with you, Ines." The glowing figure climbed into the room, wings tucked in behind him, and Rumiel stood before them, hands held wide in greeting. "At least not in that way."

"I..." Words failed her. "Of course you do. You're with Michael, remember."

"True, I stand with the Blazing Host," Rumiel said, "but that does not mean that we agree on every single measure. Please, I have come for your help, and I offer you mine in return."

With a glowing hand, he reached out toward her.

"Stay the hell away from me," she snapped, jerking away.

"I would but heal you," he said, eyes wide with sorrow. "Please, allow me to do this thing, for the love I carry for you."

"The love you..." Ines shook her head. "You're insane. All of you."

"Let him do it." Damon's voice was cold. "You and Toby need medical care, and we can't get to a hospital."

"What about you?"

"I don't think angelic magic can heal me now." He held up his right hand. Black veins ran from a circle in the center of the palm. "Isn't that right, Rumiel?"

"I would not heal a creature of the pit if I could." Rumiel spoke firmly but with tenderness. "Now please, Ines, let me help."

"Fine." She held out her arm. "But you don't touch Toby until you've proved this isn't a trick."

"Very well."

He took her injured hands in both of his. Warmth seeped from him as he began to sing in a lilting language she could not understand. It was a soothing warmth, not a burning such as had touched her before, and she felt her pain ease.

"There." Rumiel let go. "And now your brother."

As he ran his hands across Toby's face, the visible wounds disappeared. When he was done, he stepped back. Toby peeled off one of the plasters, revealing untouched skin beneath.

"My power has grown since joining with Michael on his mission." Rumiel stepped back from them all while keeping his gaze on Ines. "All of our power is growing as magic flows into your world. Yet still our goal eludes us. A righteous order slips through our fingers at every turn. Humans refuse to see the benefits that we bring. They are intent on being allowed to fight, injure, and insult each other. Few are willing to pay for their sins or to be redeemed.

"I know that I can build this better world, but I cannot do it on my own.

Nor do I remain certain that Michael's is the best course. We are too distant from humanity. We cannot make your world work for us.

"I need your help, Ines. Not just for me, but for all of humanity. Help me to build a better world."

For a long moment, she stood dumb-struck, staring at him. At last, she managed to gather the words she needed.

"You have got to be kidding." She shook her head. "You're running around judging people, causing pain and death because of some warped view of what justice is. You don't want what's best for us, any more than the rest of your Host do. What you want is for us to obey, for those you consider righteous to get inside safe little glass cages of good behavior and for the so-called sinners to suffer for their mistakes. Your people have hunted us down, nearly killed us in the name of your new order. There is no way I am helping you out."

"But Ines—"

"But nothing. Get out of here, or so help me, by God, Satan, Dawkins, or whoever is listening, I will grab one of those knives and stab you here and now."

Rumiel's face fell.

"We could save the world together," he said.

"The only person I'm interested in saving it from is you," she replied.

Rumiel turned, spread his wings, and flew away through the window.

"Surely not just him," Damon said. "I mean, there's Michael, Sanctus, the Ministry, my father..."

"Pedant." She sighed, walked over to her small pile of belongings, and started dumping them back into her bag. "This hiding thing isn't working, is it?"

Damon shook his head. "Hard to hide from magic these days."

"Then let's stop waiting for our enemies to find us." She zipped the bag shut and slung it over her shoulder. The longest knife glittered in her hand. "Let's get out there and find some of them."

CHAPTER 15
A Moment of Darkness

Finding a Ministry mage wasn't the hard part of the plan. With the streets empty, the mages would stand out even more than usual—the only people out and about who weren't soldiers or the police. Ines had counted on them being exempt from the government curfew, and that assumption paid off.

The hard part was getting around to find one.

With the curfew in place, there were no buses or trams running into the center of Manchester. Occasional cars and vans passed the travelers on their journey. These vehicles were usually in convoy, with a police car or camouflaged jeep taking up the front and rear positions.

It was a very governmental solution for getting critical people to work in a time of chaos. Some of those convoys might be doing their jobs, but others were failing.

Ines and her companions were at a junction, looking to see if there was anyone about, when they heard the sound of gunfire. They dove behind a wall as a police car hurtled down the road toward them. The siren was switched off, but the cops were racing down the road, and one of them leaned out of the passenger-side window, pointing a gun back down the street. Behind him came a jeep, two soldiers standing on the back, clinging on while they fired their assault rifles one-handed at the black-and-white car.

Half a dozen demons flocked in the air above the high-speed pursuit, cackling and rubbing their clawed hands together, swooping down to urge on the gunmen or taste the anger that drove them.

Bullets ricocheted off the pavement as the jeep hit a speed bump and the soldiers swayed wildly in the back. A chip of flying concrete brushed Ines's cheek.

Twenty seconds later, the danger was gone, both cars vanishing around a bend in the road.

"If I could meet the prime minister right now, my first words would be 'told you so.'" Damon rose from behind the wall, glancing up and down the street. "At least that will have sent anybody in the area running. Now looks like a good time to cross."

"No, wait." Ines looked back up the road in the direction the two cars had come from. "I've got another idea."

This would have been a busy road at any other time, an artery from outer residential areas into the university district, taking students from their rented houses to their lecture halls. Pubs, cafes, and newsagents made up most of the shop fronts, interspersed with the odd supermarket and, of course, more rented housing. The chase had come out of town, and Ines could see movement in the road back that way.

With the others in tow, and sticking to the cover provided by parked and abandoned cars, she made her way up the street. Walking at a crouch the whole way was uncomfortable but better than exposing herself to view for whoever was around—especially when that whoever included armed gunmen as well as angry angels.

Passing underneath a roofed pedestrian bridge between university buildings, she found herself at a large junction. There, she found what she had been looking for.

It made sense that, where possible, the Ministry would have put mages with the groups of policemen and soldiers. After all, there might not be safety in numbers right now, but there were forms of safety to be found both in guns and in magic. If the mages could protect the soldiers from demonic influences, then the soldiers could protect them from more mundane ones. That would let them patrol the streets, keeping an eye out for Ines or anyone else the Ministry considered a menace to their work.

It was a good plan, but amid the chaos unleashed by the crumbling Barrier, it had inevitably hit problems.

A police car lay on its side in the middle of the road. The car it had hit—a sleek, sporty thing with bright-yellow bodywork and a tire track up its low-sloping bonnet—was turned sideways across several lanes, its windshield shattered.

By the side of the road, policemen were restraining a man in a leather jacket and designer jeans, while a man in a gray suit sat clutching his head.

Ushering the others into hiding around the corner, Ines crept closer to the accident, making the most of the cover provided by a double-decker bus.

"You were supposed to stop this sort of thing happening," one of the policemen said to the mage.

"I can't stop anything while I'm unconscious," the mage said.

"Well, shouldn't you have seen this coming?" The policeman waved at the yellow car.

"The man was driving like an idiot, not demonically possessed." The mage rose unsteadily to his feet. "I'm equipped to deal with supernatural intrusions, not jerks and their jerk cars."

"That car's worth more than your whole life, arsehole!" the man in the leather jacket shouted.

The mage flipped him the bird with one hand while rubbing his forehead with the other. "I need to get somewhere I can rest."

"PC Fowler can escort you to safety," the policeman said. "We need to keep patrolling."

"Good grief, everyone's an idiot today," the mage said. "If you keep on without me, the demons will get to you too, just like your colleagues and those soldiers."

"Look, mate, I don't know what's going on here." The policeman failed to conceal his contempt. "But I don't believe in demons, and after this little incident, I don't much believe in you. So you can have PC Fowler go with you, or you can wander around the city by yourself. Your choice."

There was an awkward pause.

"I'll take PC Fowler," the mage said at last.

"Lucky me," one of the other cops said, shaking her head. "Come on then, sir. Let's get you home."

The mage and his escort started walking toward the junction, while the others, still restraining their prisoner, headed up the street away from Ines.

This was it, the opportunity she had been looking for. Moving as fast as she could without revealing herself, she hurried back to the junction and around the corner to Damon and Toby. In a few muttered sentences, she explained her plan.

By the time PC Fowler and her suited companion reached the junction, Toby was lying in the street underneath the footbridge, face down and groaning. Not seeing him, they turned right to head toward the center of the city. Toby let out a louder groan.

"What's that?" PC Fowler turned and squinted into the shadows where Toby lay. His theatrical moan of pain brought a smile to Ines's face where she stood hidden in the doorway of a newsagent's. Her brother was doing well, and this time not by throwing himself into danger.

"Are you all right there, kid?" Fowler walked toward Toby, her face filled with concern. She was smart enough to have pulled out her truncheon but still focused on the body in the road.

The mage followed reluctantly along behind.

"Kid?" Fowler bent to examine Toby. "It's alright, I'm a police officer. You're safe now."

As she crouched down, Damon stepped out from behind a car. It took him two long strides to reach Fowler, and in that time, she was almost upright, baton raised to block him.

She wasn't quite quick enough. Damon's right hand touched her arm, and she froze.

"Oh no, you don't." The mage threw his arms wide, weaving a magical shield between his hands. He was so focused on Damon that he didn't notice Ines emerge behind him. She grabbed his arms and yanked them back behind him, and the magic vanished. Damon clamped a hand over the man's mouth.

"We need to move," Damon said. "The spell won't hold her for long."

* * *

Someone else had broken the lock to the lecture hall, saving Ines the effort. She flung the mage down in a seat in the front row and stood over him, looming in a way she could never have done while he stood up.

"Where are the rest of the mages?" she asked.

"Who are you people?" the man said. "Let go of me. I work for the government. I can have you arrested."

"We know that." Ines's words echoed around the auditorium. So did the cracking of her knuckles as she limbered up. "We know which part of the government too. That's why you're here."

"I don't understand." The mage raised a hand. His fingers started to twitch. "Let me just—"

He yelped in pain as Ines grabbed the hand and twisted the fingers back.

"I could break these," she said. "I don't want to, but I could. And I will if you don't answer my questions."

"You're going to torture me?" The man stared at her in shock. "You bitch!"

Ines hesitated. It wasn't as though she hadn't known where her plan was heading, but she had been trying to avoid the thought. When the reality of it was presented so starkly, and with the fear any sane man would show at the thought of torture, she felt sick and angry with herself. She was about to do something horribly wrong.

"My friend had to make a terrible choice today." She nodded toward Damon while maintaining pressure on the mage's hand. "He could have continued to resist the darkness within him, to be the sort of person he wanted to be. But then things got nasty, and he realized that there was only one way to protect the people he loves. He did a dark and terrible thing, and he'll never be the same again. That's what the world has done to him, the world your people have made by unraveling the Barrier of Mercy.

"Now it's my turn. Your boss, Elizabeth Oldfield—she's taken my parents hostage. Julie and David Salgado—maybe you even know them. I don't really care whether you do or don't, because right now I'm trying very hard not to care about you.

"You see, this is my moment of darkness. Because I've seen my friend's example, and I know that, like him, I'll do anything to protect the people I love. It might scar me forever. It might turn me into someone I don't want to be. It certainly makes me a bitch, as you said. But I'll do that to protect my parents, because that's what they would do for me.

"So here's your choice. You can save me from my moment of darkness, and save yourself a lot of pain, by just telling me where Oldfield and her lackeys have based themselves in Manchester. Or we can both accept the scars of these terrible times. Of course, my scars will be emotional, while yours will be all over your face."

With her free hand, she pulled a knife from her belt.

"So tell me, shall we face my moment of darkness together?"

"MOSI." The mage looked up at her, eyes wide with terror. "The Museum of Science and Industry. Mrs. Oldfield took it over as a base of operations."

Ines let go of the mage's hand. He flinched as she leaned in and patted him on the cheek.

"Look at that, you've saved me from becoming a monster." She slid the knife away. "Now get up. We're going to lock you up in a nice solid broom cupboard Toby found. If we find out that you were lying, then I'll be back, and we'll skip this part of the conversation. If not, I'm sure someone will find you when lectures start again."

As Damon led the mage from the room at knifepoint, Ines sank trembling into one of the lecture hall seats.

"Were you really going to torture him?" Toby asked quietly.

"I don't know." Ines shook her head. She felt as though she was about to cry at the intensity of the moment and at the dreadful anger she had barely held back. "I hope not."

CHAPTER 16
This Is My Power Now

They made slow progress, ducking into side streets and alleyways to avoid patrols, hiding behind cars and in doorways from anyone who passed by. It was a strange sort of paranoia, not fearing that people were on the other side, but simply fearing that they would lose control of themselves, drawing demons or angels, creating noise that might attract the authorities. If they were to get through this alive, if they were to reach the museum, then they had to keep their heads down.

Once again, Manchester failed to live up to Ines's expectations. In her head, large cities were like the ones in films, with tight networks of side streets suitable for dodging down and foot chases. Places that would lead them through the city without being seen. Disappointingly, reality was never that simple. The centre of Manchester was intersected by broad roads, just like London, roads that would have been packed full of traffic on any other day. Roads that sliced the side streets into so many scattered stumps, forcing them to cross spaces that felt terrifyingly exposed.

Today, those streets were mostly empty. That made crossing easier. They just had to look out for the occasional speeding joyrider or military patrol. But it also made it harder to stay concealed. Sure, there were far fewer people around to see them, but they would stand out to anyone who was around. The thought alone was exhausting. The practicality of trying to stay in cover while crossing a busy street was ridiculous.

"We're just going to have to risk it." Ines looked up and down the latest wide road. Office blocks overlooked it, making it impossible to tell whether anyone was watching them.

"Wait." Damon held up a hand. "Do you hear that?"

A distant pattering turned into the approach of many feet. A voice joined them.

"Stay in line!" The response was too quiet and distant for them to make out. "I said stay in line!"

The familiar tone, laced through with recently acquired anger, made Ines's blood run cold.

"Is that Rumiel?" Damon asked.

She could only nod.

"Then we should get out of sight," Damon said.

They wriggled underneath a parked truck, bellies pressed against the cold tarmac, peering out of the shadows to see what was coming.

A crowd of people came down the street toward them. Most were dressed in shirts or blouses. Plastic identity badges hung from lanyards around their necks, the badge of the office worker. There were at least a hundred of them, some staring forward, others glancing nervously back at the angel who flew just behind them, blazing sword in hand, wings beating to keep him aloft.

A woman wobbled as her high heel gave way beneath her. Staggering out of the crowd, she leaned against a lamppost, clutching her ankle, her face white with fear. Her shoes clearly hadn't been chosen for long-distance walking, and red smears marked the toes where the skin had become badly rubbed.

"Stay in line!" Rumiel bellowed, swooping over to her. "You will come to hear the word of the Lord, to learn of this new and righteous order, or you will be punished for your sins."

"My feet," the woman whimpered, tears running down her cheeks. "Please, my feet."

In the shadows beneath the truck, Damon squirmed, bringing his right hand around in front of him. Black veins ran from the spot in his palm, glowing green at their edges. As Ines glanced at him, he looked away, glaring at Rumiel.

"Into line!" Rumiel hovered over the woman, sword raised menacingly, his expression fierce with frustration. To Ines's surprise, he didn't strike her.

"She can't, you arsehole." Another woman stepped out of the crowd. She was dressed much like the first woman— high heels, jacket and skirt, blond hair tied back. But unlike her colleague, she looked more determined than afraid. "Look at her feet. Look at her face."

"She can, and she will." This time Rumiel descended. With his empty hand, he pointed at the first woman's feet. There was a glow around them, and she blinked in surprise.

"It doesn't hurt." She peered down, voice still trembling.

"Now wipe away your tears and get back into line," Rumiel said. "Only through hearing Michael's words can you be saved. Would you rather I cut you all down for your sins?"

The woman burst into tears again. As her colleague tried to move between them, Rumiel picked her up by the neck and flung her back into the crowd. There were murmurs of misery and stifled screams, but nobody ran.

"Will you not just accept your salvation?" Rumiel yelled. Something like a tear glowed on his cheek, its light reminding Ines of how kind he could be, and of how handsome he was.

"Screw this." Damon crawled out from under the van and to his feet. Before Ines could stop him, he was striding toward Rumiel, gold watch in his left hand, the right raised as if in greeting.

"Hey you, pigeon wings!" he shouted.

"Damon?" Rumiel turned. He shook his head as if trying to dislodge an insect that had settled on his nose. "What do you want?"

"I want you to leave these people alone."

"Not only will you not help, but now you hinder me?" Rumiel rose from the ground, wings spread wide, looking like a picture from an Old Testament prophecy. "If it were not for the esteem in which Ines holds you, I would crush you here and now, demon."

Toby started crawling forward. Heart racing with terror for her brother, Ines grabbed him by the arm and hauled him back, pinning him to the ground beside her. There was no way she was letting him put himself in danger again.

"That's half-demon to you, Mr. Holier-Than-Bollocks." The fingers of Damon's hand began to twitch. "Now get away from these people."

"Get thee to Hell, abomination."

Sweeping back his wings, Rumiel hurtled toward Damon.

Damon held up both hands. The air in front of him shimmered, and Rumiel smashed into an invisible barrier.

Flinging his arms wide, Damon made the barrier visible, a gray haze in the air. As he clapped his hands together, the magic swept in upon Rumiel, and he fell like a swatted fly, crashing into the ground.

"You... What..." Rumiel rose to one knee, trembling as if he were lifting a great weight. "How..."

"This is my power now." Damon's voice was transformed, becoming a deep, menacing growl. "You think you have grown mighty? You are nothing compared with me."

Clenching his right hand into a fist, he swung it up above his head. As he did so, Rumiel was flung into the air, a chunk of the road going with him.

Where the tarmac had been, there was not empty air, but a black void that sucked in the litter from the street and bent the lamppost toward it. The woman in the high heels shrieked and clung to the lamppost as a wind threatened to suck her into that nothingness. Others in the crowd turned and ran, or fell to the ground as they struggled against its pull.

Damon looked around in alarm. As he lost focus on Rumiel, his hand spasmed. The angel went flying, disappearing over an office block. A void like the one in the street appeared around Damon's hand, and he screamed.

"What's happening?" Ines asked Toby. She was desperate to help her friend, but this was beyond her comprehension, never mind her ability to intervene.

"Too much power," Toby said. "It's overwhelming him."

Damon pressed his pocket watch against the darkness that surrounded his other hand. Swaying from side to side, the magical wind whipping his hair around, he chanted words that Ines couldn't understand. Savage-sounding words, ugly and menacing, a voice of Hell in full flow.

A chunk of the darkness broke off and disappeared into the watch, leaving the awful mass smaller. Almost immediately, it grew again, shrank again, grew again, shrank again, pulsing in size as the balance between Damon's power and his ability to control it swung back and forth.

"Can we do something?" Ines asked.

"I don't know." Toby's eyes were wide, mouth hanging open. "I do little cleansing spells and beginners' fire tricks. How would I know?"

The last of the crowd were making their escape, crawling across tarmac until they could escape the pull of the void, then staggering to their feet and running for their lives. The lamppost gave way beneath the pressure, its top half breaking free with a squeal of dying metal. It vanished into the darkness in the road.

At last, Damon seemed to get the edge in the struggle with his power. The darkness receded until it was only as large as his hand, fingers like shadows above a palm as black as night. Blood ran from his nose and the corners of his eyes as he stumbled toward the gap in the street. Sinking to his knees beside it, he plunged both hands in. The void rose up to meet him.

Ines stifled a scream as tentacles of blackness shot out and wrapped themselves around Damon. The sight of him being swallowed before her eyes filled her with dread. She couldn't bear to lose him. Not now, not ever.

This time, Toby clung to her, trying to keep her in place as she wriggled out from beneath the truck. She fought against him, knocking him back so hard, he hit a wheel. Clutching his head in shock and pain, he let go of her, and she ran out, not knowing what she could do, only that she had to do something.

Damon looked up at her, and horror filled his expression. Eyes wide with desperation, he thrust his arms deep into the mass before him and shouted in the demon tongue.

The last of the void rushed up to meet him, hitting him so hard, it flung him onto his back. As it did so, it vanished into him, and for a moment, the boy Ines loved was gone, replaced by a figure made only of shadow.

Then he opened his mouth, and the darkness rushed forth, streaming out of him, a black pillar punching up into the sky. His hands appeared, then his feet in their smart black shoes. Arms, legs, body, and finally face emerged as the last of the darkness rushed out of him and disappeared into the clouds far above.

As Ines rushed to his side, Damon forced himself up on his elbows. Blood crusted on his face, and his eyes were red rimmed. Patches of hair were twisted up as if singed by a flame. Every little movement made him wince.

"That was the second-worst thing I've ever done," he croaked. "Right after betting I could down half a pint of vodka."

"You idiot." Ines wrapped her arms around him. He winced but hugged her back.

"It seems I've bitten off more than I can chew." He eased her away and looked down at his hand. The spot was still there, and black veins covered more of his skin than before.

"I don't care." Ines took his face between her hands and kissed him, tenderly at first then with desperation as great as she had felt at nearly losing him.

"I thought you didn't want to—" Damon began but was cut short when she kissed him again.

At last, she pulled away and helped him to his feet. Toby stood nearby, looking down at his shoes.

"Losing you would have destroyed me," she said. "From now on, I'm keeping you as close as I can."

CHAPTER 17
The Ministry in the Museum

"They could be in any of those buildings." Ines looked out of a shop front, down a tree-lined pedestrian street to the Museum of Science and Industry. The shop had been looted, as had several along this road, and no one had come to board up the broken windows. Broken glass formed jagged teeth around the openings, making Ines feel as though she were about to be swallowed by a concrete monster.

Perhaps she was. Perhaps there were demons who could disguise themselves as retail outlets, or mages who could bring buildings to life. That was the problem with not knowing magic—she didn't know what couldn't be done, what was worth fearing, and what should be ignored. Each day seemed to bring some new and terrible development, like the void that had almost overwhelmed Damon. It was impossible to be ready for everything. The best she could do was accept the reality of whatever happened and then fight it as hard as she could.

"So where do we start?" Damon spoke softly, exhausted as well as trying to avoid detection.

The museum consisted of several buildings. The main one was a mixture of old-fashioned red brick and modern glass, with chrome touches that seemed to hint at the coming future. Across the road was a glass building like the gleaming pavilions of a great Victorian fair, but with its windows tall and narrow or covered in bars. It looked like what happened when the first railway stations grew up. Despite its appearance, it wasn't the building most likely to house a train. Two bars of mobile Internet access had been enough to access the museum's webpage, revealing that engines were in the Power Hall—a broad, low building, again in red brick, that housed machines intended to impress excitable children and the businessmen who hired it out for corporate functions.

"The Power Hall looks easiest to get into." Ines pointed to the building. "The toilets are out back of it, so there must be an out-of-the-way door to get to them. With any luck, they won't have thought to guard the route to the loo."

"What are we going to do once we get inside?" Toby asked.

"Improvise," Ines replied. "If we can, I'd like to grab another mage for questioning—one who's been spending time around Elizabeth and might know where they're holding Mum and Dad. But it'll depend on what we find inside."

"Maybe Mum and Dad are in there." Toby's expression brightened.

"Maybe." Ines wasn't going to risk too much hope. "Let's find out."

Getting around to the back of the Power Hall took a detour through nearby streets as they tried to stay hidden from any Ministry lookouts. There was a back door, as Ines had predicted, but it was locked and solid looking.

"I've got this." Damon reached out, but Ines grabbed his hand before he could touch the door.

"You're not going to use your magic again, are you?" she asked.

"How else are we going to get in?" He frowned grimly.

"The same way any self-respecting teenager would." Ines glanced at a window above the door. "Breaking and entering."

"If you break a window, they'll hear it."

"Better that than putting you at risk again." She took his hand. "You could barely contain that power earlier, and now it's weakened you. Do you really think you can safely do magic?"

"Ines, please. I just want to—"

"Got it." There was a smell of burning wood, and the glowing door handle came away in Toby's hand, bring the whole lock with it. He grinned then yelped and dropped the red-hot metal, waving his hand about. "Ow, ow, ow!"

"Good job, Toby." Damon smiled. Ines tried not to worry about what the magic might be doing to her little brother.

The door swung open, and they stepped inside.

The interior of the Power Hall was as impressive as the museum's publicity had promised. Entire steam engines sat next to old factory machinery, inner workings exposed, gleaming in the sunlight spilling through the windows. Vast geared wheels sat idle between the brick pillars, but all looked as if they could spring into action at any moment.

"This is so cool." Toby's whisper echoed around the deserted gallery.

"No sign of mages." Ines led them toward the center of the room, looking around to see what other doors there were, where else people might be. The hall was as silent as a mouse. Not even their footsteps echoed back to her across the cavernous room.

She tensed. Their footsteps should have echoed.

"This isn't right." She drew a knife.

"How very observant," a voice said from the emptiness.

The air shimmered in front of her, and a mage appeared. His teeth were gritted, his hands trembling as he held them in front of him. Then he lowered his hands, sagging with relief as a dozen of his colleagues appeared around the room.

Every way Ines turned, she saw a gray-suited figure wearing dark glasses. Two stood between her and the door she had come in through. They raised their hands, batons of blue magical force extending from each right fist, shields of power appearing on their left arms. Others cast the same spells or raised their hands, fingers twitching as they murmured incantations and prepared to launch spells.

"Please surrender." The voice was Tamsin Shaw's, but Ines couldn't see her among the assembled mages. She wondered if Shaw remained concealed or if she was projecting her voice from elsewhere in the museum. Perhaps it wasn't even magic, just the PA system. "None of us wants to see you three hurt or these venerable machines damaged."

Ines took a deep breath. Shaw's reasonable tone, far from calming her, added to her anger at the Ministry of Occult Affairs and its mages. If they were so reasonable, then they had reasonably chosen to behave in the worst way possible— kidnapping her parents, endangering her brother, putting the whole world in peril. They could have done anything with their magic, and they had chosen this.

She understood now what it meant to see red. Fury clouded her thoughts, and she felt the blood pounding in her temples. Her face flushed, cheeks burning with heat that no amount of reason could quench. The urge to attack the mages was almost uncontrollable.

Toby raised his hands, fingers trembling as he prepared to start weaving spells. Damon pulled out his watch and turned to cover her back, the strain of every movement clear in his face.

If she put them in danger like this, would she be any better than Shaw and the rest? Hesitating, she lowered her blade.

"I'm glad to see we can all be reasonable," Shaw's disembodied voice said.

As the calm of those words reached her, Ines made her decision.

Fire flashing in her heart, she lunged at the nearest mage.

That first attack was planned, a precision strike that forced the mage to raise his shield and let her slip underneath, grabbing his arm and twisting him around until he screamed.

After that, there was no calculation, just finely honed instincts. Ines gave in to her rage.

Leaping and lunging, kicking and punching, she moved among the mages, attacking anyone within reach. Muscle memory guided her as she swept the legs out from beneath one of her enemies then grabbed another and flung him to the ground. Blasts of magic sizzled past her head. Weapons of pure will missed her by precious inches. There were screams of pain and of anger, grunts and groans, thuds and cracks.

Somewhere in the brawl, she lost her knife, leaving it buried in someone's thigh. Blood dripped from her fist as she punched a mage with long red hair and bright lipstick. She slammed her elbow into someone coming at her from behind, ducked beneath a magical club, and rolled clear as it smashed the floor at her feet.

As she rose, something flashed toward her. She ducked, but her opponent was luckier or more gifted than the rest. A magical club caught the side of her head.

A bright flash filled the world, and she reeled with pain.

Ines was half-blind and staggering, but her instincts were still strong. She heard as much as saw someone coming for her and dived clear. As vision returned, she rolled beneath an old steam engine, railway tracks battering her side as she did so, then scrambled out the far side into a narrow space between the train and the wall.

She needed something, anything to give her an edge. Seeing a toolbox in the shadows beside the train, she grabbed a screwdriver in one hand and a hammer in the other.

The redheaded mage came around the corner of the train. Blood dripped from her nose. Between her fingers, she wove a net of pure light.

"You're going down, you little bitch," she hissed.

Ines charged toward the mage. After only two strides, dizziness overtook her. She stumbled, legs tangling, bounced off the wall, and managed to keep herself upright, momentum carrying her forward.

The mage swung her net. Ines raised her hammer, catching it among the bright strands. The net became tangled but was still falling toward her. Jerking the hammer, she flung it away, let her feet slide out from under her, and skidded forward. The net landed somewhere behind her as she smashed into the mage's shins, and the two of them tumbled together on the ground.

The woman fought like a demon— kicking, scratching, biting, twisting. Though shorter by half a foot, Ines flipped her over, pinning her to the floor, even as nails gouged her cheek. She pressed the sharp tip of the screwdriver against the underside of the mage's chin.

"Stop that, or I'll stick this in and stir your brains around," Ines said.

The woman went still.

"Good." Ines kept the screwdriver in place. "Now we're both going to stand up slowly. You're fast, but so am I. Try anything funny, and I'll drive this right up into your brain."

They rose, and Ines slid around behind her captive, shifting the screwdriver to her other hand, keeping it in place. They emerged from behind the train.

"Everybody stop," Ines yelled.

Peering around the taller woman, she saw that Toby and Damon had been driven back into a corner by three of the mages. They probably would have been captured if so many hadn't been busy dealing with Ines. That made her smile, despite the stinging of her cheek and the spinning of her head.

Everybody looked at her—Damon, Toby, the mages around them, those she had left lying injured across the hall.

"What's your name?" she asked, applying more pressure with the screwdriver.

"Karen," her captive replied. "Karen Riley."

"The rest of you listen," Ines said. "You're going to let me and my friends go. If you don't, I'll kill Karen here." She meant it as a bluff, but the fire raging in her belly told her she might be able to do it. "Step back, all of you."

"Do as she says." Shaw's voice still came from out of nowhere. If she was in the room, then Ines had no idea where.

The mages stepped away from Toby and Damon but kept their weapons raised.

Ines walked slowly forward around the fallen.

"I tried to be reasonable," Shaw said. "Remember that."

With those last few words, the voice coalesced, coming from somewhere behind Ines. She turned to look, but it was too late. A hand grabbed her shoulder, and her whole body went numb. The screwdriver clattered on the floor. As she fell beside it, she saw the mages closing in on Damon and Toby. Then the whole world faded away.

CHAPTER 18
United in Misery

The first thing Ines was aware of was the ticking of a clock. Each tick in turn snagged the edge of her mind, drawing her a little closer to consciousness.

She took a deep breath, trying to muster the energy to open her eyes and face the world. The smell of her own body assailed her—sweat, grime, and stale blood. How had she gotten into this state, she wondered. And if she smelled this bad, how awful must she look?

Stretching out her fingers, she felt a carpet beneath her, the short, hard-wearing sort used in offices and public buildings. She was lying on it, with something else supporting her head.

Tensing herself, ready to fight whatever mages were near, she opened her eyes.

Toby smiled nervously at her. His face was upside down, and it took her a moment to realize that was because her head was in his lap.

"You're okay!" He leaned over in an attempt to hug her. "I mean, you are okay, aren't you?"

Ines rolled her head slowly from side to side. She'd expected aches, or at the very least stiffness, after the workout the fight had put her whole body through. Instead, she felt clear, almost refreshed.

"I think so." She sat up, but that set her head spinning, so she sank back into her brother's lap.

Damon sat beside them, a cheap office wall clock on the floor in front of him. His fingers were splayed across its clear plastic cover, its hands jerking beneath his as the seconds ticked by. There was a gleam in his eye. Strain showed on his crumpled forehead.

"Are you casting magic?" Ines asked, alarmed at the sight.

Letting out a long breath, Damon set the clock aside.

"Just a little," he said. "To help you revive, and to try to get control of my power again."

"You could have been killed!" This time she sat up successfully. "After what happened—"

"After what happened, I need to ease back into it slowly. That's what I'm doing." He reached out and squeezed her hand. "I can do this."

"If you say so." She could hear the doubt in her voice.

"Really, I can," Damon said.

Ines let it go. She was in no position to criticize anyone for overconfidence. She'd led them into a trap and gotten them all captured.

They were being held in what looked like a small meeting room. There were half a dozen chairs around a rectangular table, a telephone in the middle of the table and a monitor fixed to the wall. The only other feature was a print of an abstract painting hanging opposite the door, and the only illumination came from the ceiling lights.

Ines stood and leaned over the table. Picking up the phone receiver, she pressed it to her ear. Silence greeted her—no dial tone. Slamming the phone back down, she stalked to the door and gripped the handle. It only moved half an inch before hitting some obstruction outside. However hard she wrenched at it, the door wouldn't budge. She kicked it, as much to punish herself as the disobedient door.

"It's not your fault," Damon said. He was sitting at the table now, his watch in one hand and a ten-pence coin in the other. He spun the coin on the table top. The air around it shimmered, and for a moment, the coin stopped in place. Then the shimmering spilled out across the table. Damon snatched back his hand, and the coin kept on spinning.

"Then whose fault is it?" Ines snapped. "I led us into this mess. I failed to fight them off."

"None of us fought them off." Toby dug a chocolate bar out of his pocket, the wrapper battered, the whole thing bent in the middle.

"But I'm the one who knows how to fight," Ines said. "I'm the strong one, and the one with the knives. I'm your big sister. I have to protect you."

"You're doing the best you can."

"And it's not good enough!" She slammed her fist into the wall. The coin rattled onto the table as Damon again lost control of his spell. Toby paused in opening his chocolate bar. "I'm getting us out of here, and then I'm finding someone else to look after you. It's the only way you can be safe."

"I'm not staying behind while you two go off on adventures." Toby stood and glared at her, the chocolate forgotten. "You're not Mum. You don't get to decide what happens to me."

"Adventures?" Ines said. "People are dying around us. This isn't an adventure—it's a nightmare. Stop acting like a little brat."

"You're the brat," Toby said. "Not just a brat, a b—"

"Enough!" Damon shouted. The air shimmered all around the table, black tendrils spreading out all around him. He grimaced as he clenched his fingers, and the tendrils disappeared, but tiny black veins still crisscrossed the back of his hand. "You're both just trying to look after each other. Surely you can talk like that's what you want?"

Ines hung her head. He was right. She wanted to keep Toby and Damon safe, but that kept getting out of hand. And the harder she tried to look after them, the worse things got and the more miserable she felt. Those feelings held her back, made it hard to think straight. As long as she was just thinking about herself, she could get by, but this was too much.

"There's only one way I can look after us all." She took a deep breath, looking at each of them in turn—the most important boys in her life. "I have to go on alone."

"What?" Their voices rose as one in indignation.

"I love you both," she said. "And you've helped me get this far. But looking after you is holding me back. Someone needs to find Mum and Dad and to stop these lunatics. I can do that better on my own."

"You arrogant, pig-headed, ridiculous woman." Damon rose to his feet. As he did so, he knocked his chair over, but instead of falling to the floor, it hung in the air behind him, caught in a shimmer of magical power that filled the air. Black tendrils crept once more from his hands, but he ignored them, his attention entirely on Ines. "After everything we've been through together, do you really think you can do this better without me?"

"Yes." Ines folded her arms across her chest and looked him in the eye, trying to ignore the hurt she saw there. Were there black veins creeping from the corners of his eyes now too? It didn't matter. Once they were apart, he could stop dabbling with the magic that was doing him so much harm.

"I saved you from a demon," he said. "From lots of demons. And from mages."

"You nearly got killed facing Rumiel," Ines said. "How does that help me?"

"I can protect you from him. Once I've got control again, I can do that."

"Protect me?" Ines steeled herself. What came next would hurt him, but it was for his own good. "Rumiel's stronger than you, Damon. More powerful. Beating him almost destroyed you, and that was when you had the advantage of surprise. Do you really think you can beat him again?"

"Oh, so that's what this is about." Damon's voice went cold and hard. "Rumiel."

Silence fell. Ines stared at Damon. He wasn't the only one hurting. The tone of his voice froze her. She felt as though a rock had been dropped into the pit of her stomach.

"What do you mean?" she whispered.

"Rumiel's more powerful," Damon said bitterly, black veins spreading across his eyes, the air darkening around him. "Rumiel's stronger. Rumiel's prettier. Rumiel's a better damn kisser."

"I never—" This time it wasn't Ines's own feelings that cut her words short. It was Damon's power spilling across the room, holding everything in place. The ticking of the clock slowed to a halt.

"Of course you prefer Rumiel," Damon said. "What girl wouldn't? He's all muscles and smiles, with that carefully crafted hair and those trendy clothes. It's easy to look fashionable when it's all just imaginary, an extension of your will. Fit, blond, charming, he's a poster boy for pretty retards the world over.

"Oh, and he's part of the armies of light, isn't he? None of this ugly demonic taint on him." Damon waved his hands in front of his face, black tendrils floating around them. "Just pure glowing power, the better to smite the unrighteous and win over the impressionable."

Every word was like a dagger stabbing at Ines. She wanted Damon. Hadn't she shown that? Hadn't she told him that? What more could she do?

A small part of her recognised the kernel of truth within what Damon was saying. There was no denying that she had been attracted to Rumiel. Something still stirred inside her when she saw him. But those feelings were nothing compared with what she and Damon had been through together. Surely he could see that?

Feeling as if she were fighting through quicksand, she forced her mouth open.

"I don't want Rumiel," she said. "I want you."

Damon snorted. His eyes were entirely black now, the air around him a gray haze.

"And I don't want to be second best to that pompous twat." Damon's voice wasn't his own. It was low, rasping, and vicious, like something that had crawled out of the pits of Hell. "But we can't all have what we want. You chose me because he isn't here. That doesn't mean I have to accept your choice."

"What do you mean?" Ines asked, knowing the answer all too well. She needed to hear him say it, to grasp at the slim chance that she might have misunderstood, or that he might change his mind.

"I mean there's nothing between us." Damon grabbed the chair hanging in the air behind him. He pushed it back against the wall and sat down, arms folded. The shimmering receded, but the black remained in his eyes. "Once this is over, I never want to see you again."

Without the magic holding her in place, Ines slumped against the wall. Her muscles had turned to water, all her physical and emotional strength exhausted. There was nothing left to hold her up. Every fiber of her being trembled.

A sob emerged from a corner of the room. Toby sat curled up around himself, tears streaming down his face. When she caught his eye, she saw pain, but anger too, and he quickly looked away, wiping his cheeks with the back of his hand.

Toby's sniffing was the only sound to be heard as they sat in their separate corners, staring at the floor. Toby's sniffing and the hands of the clock ticking around and around.

CHAPTER 19
The Revelation of Tamsin Shaw

It was half an hour before Ines heard any other signs of life. A miserable half an hour in which she sat brooding on everything she had said and heard, seen and done. Half an hour of trying to imagine a way to break out, a mental task made more difficult by trying not to involve Toby in the plan, and by the uncertainty that now hung over Damon.

Even thinking about him was hard after what he had said, but the thoughts were inescapable. A lump rose in her throat whenever she looked up and saw him sitting on the other side of the room, as silent as she was.

At last, the terrible quiet was broken by footsteps approaching along the corridor outside. Forcing herself to her feet, Ines stood against the wall next to the door. If she caught someone by surprise as they came in, maybe she could get hold of a hostage. Then they would have something to bargain with.

There was a clattering as their captors removed the blockages outside. If this room could be locked, then the Ministry mages clearly didn't have the key and had to make do with an improvised barricade to secure the prisoners. The handle turned, and the door swung. Ines tensed, ready for action.

"I'm not a complete idiot, Miss Salgado," Tamsin Shaw said from the other side of the doorway. "Please move to where I can see you."

Ines hesitated. Did she even want to let Shaw in to talk?

But then how was anything going to change if they stayed locked up in here?

She crossed the room and stood between Damon and Toby, facing Shaw from against the far wall.

Shaw stood in the doorway, straight faced beneath her dark glasses, a tray in her hands. Four more mages stood behind her, all of them in matching suits of the same style and same shade of gray.

"My colleagues won't be coming in with me," Shaw said. "But they'll be out here waiting, and if they need to come in, then they have orders not to hold back."

"Were you holding back in the Power Hall?" Ines asked.

"Do you want to find out?" Shaw said.

Ines glared at the mages. Maybe she could rush them and try to break out into the corridor. At her best, that would have been hard, and she felt exhausted physically as well as emotionally. After a moment's contemplation, she shrugged.

That was enough for Shaw. She stepped into the room. One of the other mages closed the door behind her, leaving the four of them alone.

"It's thirsty work, fighting." Shaw placed the tray on the table then whipped a cloth off the top, revealing cans of drink and a pile of sandwiches in bright cardboard wrappers. "And I dread to think how long it's been since you kids had a decent meal."

"I'm not a kid," Ines snapped. "Neither is Damon."

Shaw pulled a chair out and sank into it. With slow, careful movements, she took off her dark glasses, put them away in her pocket, and folded her hands on the table in front of her.

"How old are you, Ines?" she asked. "Fifteen? Sixteen?"

"I'm nearly seventeen," Ines said.

"I was still a kid when I was seventeen." Shaw opened a can of cola and took a long gulp. Then she looked back at Ines. Her eyes were bloodshot around the edges, and there were dark bags beneath them. "Not that I realized it at the time. Maybe you're different. But I bet you're still hungry."

When Ines just glared at her, Shaw turned her attention to Toby.

"How about you?" She held out a sandwich.

Toby looked at Ines with the same expression he used to get new toys out of their parents.

"What do we have to do for the food?" Ines asked.

"Nothing," Shaw replied. "I'm not going to starve a bunch of kids, however violent you've proved yourselves to be. But I will talk to you about what's going on and ask some questions."

"What if we don't want to listen to you?"

"Then you'll have to find a way to eat with your fingers in your ears." Shaw opened a pack of sandwiches. "I'll give you a moment to decide what to do, but it seems like a no-brainer to me."

She started on a sandwich, barely pausing to chew before she swallowed each bite.

It didn't seem as if there were really any options. Ines nodded to Toby, and the two of them pulled out chairs.

"No," Damon said, his raw anger making Ines flinch.

Black tendrils shot from his watch as he held it outstretched before him.

Dropping her food, Shaw held up her hands. The air in front of her turned hazy, and the tips of the tendrils faded out before they reached her. Her pale-blue eyes narrowed, and she twisted her lips, straining to hold back the force of Damon's attack. Then the air between her and the door pulsed, and she seemed to gain strength. She rose to her feet, dark tentacles dissolving before her. Damon's power retreated, inch by inch, back toward him. He grimaced then lowered his hands, and the magic faded away.

"No need to come in," Shaw said as someone pounded on the door. "Watchword dodo."

"Very good, Ms. Shaw," someone called from the corridor.

"I understand why you did that." Shaw kept her eyes on Damon as she sat back down. "But please, let's at least try talking."

Glowering, Damon flung himself into a seat and ripped open a sandwich packet.

"What are you hoping to achieve?" Shaw asked, looking at each of them in turn.

"To get Mum and Dad back," Toby said, his defiance making Ines smile. "And stop your... your... whatever it is you're doing."

"You think you can do that?" Shaw raised an eyebrow. "How about you?" She turned to Ines. "Do you think he can do that?"

"My brother's better than any of you," Ines said.

"Tough talk for a prisoner," Shaw said. "Which side are you on, anyway? First you're running around with an angel, now a demon."

"Half demon," Damon said.

"Which makes him more human than most of you lot," Ines added.

Out of the corner of her eye, she saw Damon smile.

"As my grandfather would say, you really are full of piss and vinegar." Shaw rubbed her eyes. "Of course, others might say that you're full of shit, even if it's remarkably courageous shit."

"Better that than be full of selfishness and lust for power," Ines said.

"Don't presume to know me." Shaw finished her drink and tossed the can into a bin in the corner of the room. "As for you, I've heard enough. We're keeping you here until this business is over. I'll arrange bedding, clean clothes, things like that. There'll be a rota for taking you to the loo."

"What if I need to wee sooner?" Toby stuck out his lower lip.

"You told me you're not kids. I'm sure you can hold it in."

That was the moment when Ines felt something break inside of her. She could cope with the insults and the anger. Even the idea that they would be kept captive didn't faze her. They'd gotten out of difficult situations before. They could find a way. Captivity was some abstract problem they would deal with.

But the details made it real. They weren't being let out of this room, never mind the Ministry's grasp. She imagined someone handing them sleeping bags and bundles of clothes the wrong size, more packaged meals on trays like this one. Only being let out one at a time, for long enough to use the toilet and no more, half a dozen mages escorting them back and forth. Faced with concrete reality, her resolve crumbled, and she slumped in her seat. Resignedly, she started eating a cheese sandwich. Only as she chewed the first mouthful did she realize how hungry she had let herself get.

Shaw's expression softened.

"It isn't just about stopping you," the mage said. "I know you think you're a big menace, but there are far worse people out there. The cities are turning into war zones. Most of the police forces have opened up their weapon caches and started arming ordinary bobbies to back up the tactical aid units. The gangs have done the same, getting every gun they can onto the streets. Some of the army units have started shooting to kill, and they're fighting the police almost as often as they're fighting the gangs. That's not even getting into the lone nutcases and violent opportunists. I don't care what the minister says—this is as much about keeping you kids safe as it is about containing you."

Maybe it was the improvement that food brought, or maybe it was Shaw's sympathetic tone. Either way, Ines felt her spirits lift. Maybe there was an opening here.

"You don't agree with what Oldfield's doing?" she asked.

"I didn't say that," Shaw replied. "Just that I take a different view on you. We're here to serve, after all."

"You didn't deny it." Damon leaned forward, fixing his dark gaze on Shaw. "You disagree with Oldfield."

Shaw frowned.

"I believe in what the Ministry is doing," she said. "I've spent my whole working life dealing with the fallout from demons and angels meddling in people's lives. We need to end that, to give people more freedom to make their own choices. That's what Minister Oldfield is leading us towards."

"By kidnapping my mum and dad?" Toby looked so convincingly shocked, if Ines hadn't been his sister, she might never have known that he was deliberately acting up. "That's the opposite of making people free. So is this!"

He flung a half-empty can of cola down in exaggerated disgust.

"It's for the best." Shaw put on her dark glasses and stood, looking down at them. "Nobody is perfect, but the minister is doing important work. I believe in her."

"I don't believe you," Ines said. "If you thought she was right, then you wouldn't be here, worrying about keeping a bunch of kids comfortable when there's a world to be remade."

"Believe what you want," Shaw said. "As long as you're here, it doesn't matter."

"But what about Mum and Dad?" Toby whimpered. "Where are they? Have you killed them?"

"They're alive. I don't know about your mother, but I saw your father half an hour ago, and he was perfectly well."

"He's here?" Ines jumped up.

"Only for another"—Shaw looked at the clock—"hour, then he'll be on his way to Newcastle. I'm afraid you won't be managing any dramatic midnight rescues, or whatever fairy-tale plan you're dreaming up."

She opened the door, revealing the mages in the corridor, their hands raised ready for trouble.

"Eat as much as you want." Shaw nodded to the food on the table. "But don't drink too much. You'll have to wait until your father's on that train before I let you out of here to use the toilet."

Then she was gone, closing the door behind her.

Toby's expression turned into a massive grin.

"Dad's here!" He grabbed hold of Ines's hand. "That's brilliant! Now we have to find a way out. You can find a way out, can't you?"

Ines stared at the table, trying to think of any answer she could believe in.

"We can," Damon said. "We just need to work out how."

Ines looked up. They were working together again. Things didn't seem quite too bleak.

CHAPTER 20
Paved With Good Intentions

"Maybe if we rattle the door handle, it'll shake something loose?" Toby said, spitting sandwich crumbs. "I mean, like, really rattle it a lot."

"It's not a bad idea," Ines said, lying to keep her brother's spirits up. "But I think whoever's outside might notice and put stuff back."

"Oh." Toby nodded. "Yeah, you're right."

He reached for a can of lemonade.

"I can use my power," Damon said. "We just need to work out how."

An all-too-familiar tension tightened Ines's guts. She set aside her half-eaten sandwich.

"Can you control it?" She looked him in the eye. Black veins still showed there and across the backs of his hands. His voice had a hoarse quality, like a saw scraping against concrete. It set her teeth on edge. "After what happened before. When..."

She didn't want to say it out loud. If she talked about what had happened, then that would make what he had said real, and she couldn't face that. Not yet.

"I was born to such power." Arrogance from Damon wasn't new, but the tone of it was different—more grandiose, less cut with sly humour. "Do you doubt my ability to wield it?"

"It's not wielding it that's the problem," Ines said. "It's controlling it. And you haven't managed that so far."

"I will control it." He frowned. The black veins receded a little, and his old voice returned. "Sooner or later, I'm going to have to try."

He looked so nervous, she wanted to reach out and take his hand, to tell him it would all be okay. Instead, she pushed her hand in the other direction, picked up her sandwich, and took a bite. Using eating to buy herself time, she mustered her thoughts. Once the sandwich was finished, she spoke again.

"What sort of things could you do?" she asked. "Does it still have to relate to time somehow, or is the power your father sent to you different?"

"I'm not entirely sure." He took his watch from his pocket and started winding it. "It could be—"

He jerked his head up and looked around.

"Did you hear that?" he asked.

"I don't—" A muffled voice caught Ines's attention. Somewhere in the nearby rooms, someone was shouting. Then there was a crash. "Is that fighting?"

She went to the door and pressed her ear against it. Footsteps raced down the corridor. There was more shouting and a crackling sound.

"This could be our chance." She grabbed the door handle and twisted it frantically back and forth. "If we can shake something loose."

"Like I said!" Toby stuffed a sandwich into his pocket and went to stand beside her.

"Never mind shaking things loose." Damon took the framed picture off the wall and handed it to Ines. "That's a cheap, flimsy door, probably hollow inside. If we don't mind making a noise..."

Ines grinned. "Right now, who'll notice?"

She gripped the picture in both hands and swung it sideways at the door as hard as she could. The impact jolted her arms right up to the shoulders. Where the metal frame had hit, the door was already splintering. On the second blow, the wood gave way with a crack, and the third hit left a hole large enough for her to wriggle her fingers into. She snapped off thin pieces of wooden board, enlarging the gap. Half a minute later, she was reaching through the hole, splintered edges jabbing at her arm, and pushing away the chair jammed beneath the door handle. Hot air lapped unexpectedly at her hand.

A point of wood gouged Ines's arm as she withdrew it. Wincing, she looked down and saw a little blood staining her hoodie.

There were bigger things to worry about right now.

The corridor outside barely registered in Ines's mind. Her entire attention was drawn by the larger hall at the end and the blazing inferno consuming one side of it. A dozen figures were illuminated by the firelight. Some were in gray suits soaked with sweat, magic crackling from their fingers. A smaller number were clad in immaculate white, weapons glowing in their hands, wings spread wide behind them.

At the center of the chilling tableau, the angel Michael hovered amid the flames. His white hair fluttered in the hot air rising from the fire. His eyes, normally cold and sharp as diamonds, burned so brightly that they hurt look at, even at such a distance.

"Burn them all," Michael roared. "Purge this world with fire and blade!"

As Ines and her companions stood staring in horror, one of the angels broke clear. She flew toward them, wings brushing the sides of the corridor.

"You!" she screamed, hurling a spear.

Ines flung herself at Toby, dragging him to the ground. There was a thud and a yell of pain. She looked up in fear at Damon, but he was unhurt.

Behind them were three mages. One was slumped against the wall, blood streaming from around the spear that had skewered his shoulder. Another flung a magical net, while the third raised a club of glowing power.

As the mages and the angel charged each other, Ines rolled out beneath their legs. Toby followed, and Damon dashed after them, ducking as the angel swung a sword in a wide arc.

Together, they ran down the corridor and burst through a door at the end. They were back in the museum's public space, amid displays about Victorian Manchester and the march of technology. Long-dead laborers gazed out from black-and-white photos, while behind them, powerful machines stood frozen in history's gaze.

"Come on." Ines led the other two through the hall and down a staircase.

They tumbled out into the entrance hall just as a familiar figure strode into view.

Like the other angels, Rumiel stood in the full majesty of his power. Wings were spread wide behind him, a sword of fire blazed in his hand, and a golden corona of light surrounded his face. Beyond him, visible through the doors and windows of the museum, more angels fought against the Ministry's mages. None shone as brightly or drew Ines's attention so completely as Rumiel.

"We are here to save you," Rumiel bellowed at the mage backing away from him. "Set aside your fight and accept salvation."

The mage raised trembling hands, a shield of magic spreading before him.

"Can you not understand this simple thing?" Rumiel's face was crumpled in frustration. "Do you wish to be damned?"

He raised his sword but did not charge as other angels were doing. He seemed to be waiting, listening for the response of a man unable to muster words, a man too consumed by terror to consider a response.

Ines looked at the fighting outside and listened to Toby panting beside her, already exhausted. It would take a miracle to get him through that melee alive, and she didn't expect her prayers to be answered anytime soon. Not with the likes of Michael and Rumiel as Heaven's servants.

Except that Michael and Rumiel weren't quite the same. She thought back to the figure in the flames, promising to purge the world with bloodshed, and compared him with the angel in front of her. For all the threat he represented, Rumiel was still trying to save rather than destroy those he thought had gone wrong.

Perhaps what passed for her prayers had been answered after all.

"Rumiel," she called out, walking tentatively towards him.

"What are you doing?" Damon hissed, but Ines ignored him.

"Rumiel," she said again.

He turned to look at her. A surprised smile lit up his face in a way that the glow of heavenly power or of flames never could.

"Ines!" he exclaimed. "Have you come to join us?"

"The Ministry had us captive." She gestured toward Damon and Toby. "We just want to get out of here alive. Can you help?"

The mage turned and ran. Rumiel seemed indifferent, his attention entirely upon her.

"Of course," he said. "Repent your sins, join our side, and you and your brother will be quite safe."

"There's Damon too," Ines said. "And we don't want to join the fighting, just to get out."

Rumiel glared past her at Damon.

"I will not give aid to Hell spawn," he said. "Nor to those who still resist the will of Heaven." He stepped back, raising his sword again. "Still you defy the righteous!"

"Please, Rumiel." Ines held out her hands. "I'm begging you, we just need—"

Something grabbed her body, an invisible force like a giant fist. Panic gripped her as she realized that her arms were pinned to her sides. Invisible claws pressed against her neck.

"Grab the children," a stern voice called out. "Strike group, kill the angel."

Half a dozen gray-clad mages rushed out of a doorway. At their head, prowling across the room in a pinstripe suit, was Elizabeth Oldfield. Her hand was outstretched towards Ines, curled up as if grasping an invisible doll.

Rumiel leapt into the air, wings spread wide as he soared above the mages. He dodged a blast of magical energy, smashed another aside with his sword, and swept down upon Oldfield.

Fast as lightning, the minister brought her hands around. Rumiel slammed into a wall of pure magical force and slid to the ground.

As Oldfield moved her hands, Ines felt the grip on her vanish.

Three of the mages closed in on Rumiel, while three more headed towards Damon and Toby. Damon pulled out his watch and began chanting then staggered back as a writhing mass of black tentacles burst from his arm. One of the mages was knocked flying, while the tentacles enveloped a second.

The third mage reached Toby. Flames leapt from the boy's fingertips, only to be quenched as the mage summoned water out of thin air.

This was what Ines had feared—being around her was again putting her brother in danger. She ran screaming at the mage, who turned just in time for her fist to hit him in the face. He grunted, blood running from his lips. Then she hooked a leg around behind his and knocked him from his feet. He hit the ground headfirst and lay still.

"Stay with Damon," Ines said.

"OK," Toby replied, his head bobbing up and down in a startled nod.

In the center of the hall, Rumiel and Oldfield stood face to face. Glowing paws like those of a lion extended from her hands, claws unsheathed as they locked around his sword. The rest of the mages lay scattered on the ground.

The combatants swayed and staggered as each tried to push their weapons toward the other's face. The power of Oldfield's magic and Rumiel's strength was closely matched, but not perfectly so. Slowly but surely, the minister was driving Rumiel's flaming blade back towards his face.

Looking once more through the doors to the street, Ines saw that the battle between mages and angels continued. Trying to fight their way through that was a dreadful thought. Becoming a prisoner of the mages again was almost as bad, and a near certainty if Oldfield, with all her power, was free to stop them.

That left one option, the least awful of a bad bunch.

All of Ines's knives had been taken when they were captured. She raised her fists and ran straight at Elizabeth Oldfield.

The minister turned as Ines approached, swiping at her with a claw. Ines rolled beneath the attack, ending in a crouch behind Oldfield.

Rumiel, now faced with only half of Oldfield's power, pushed with all his might. Oldfield staggered back, fell over Ines, and sprawled on the ground.

"Ha! Look what we can achieve together." Rumiel grinned at Ines then raised his sword above Oldfield.

"Imagine how much more we could achieve." Ines grabbed Rumiel's arm. "You want to save people, but Michael just wants to destroy them. Work with us, and you really could make the world a better place, not just a burned-out one."

Rumiel frowned then looked up at the sound of footfalls. Oldfield was up and running from the room.

"I let her get away!" the angel said.

"Help us get away," Ines said. "Do something good to balance the bad."

Smoke was drifting down the stairs along with the battle songs of Michael's fearsome host. Outside the doors, fighting continued while the museum burned, its wonders and learning turning to ash.

Rumiel hesitated then grabbed hold of Ines, pulling her close to him. With three great beats of his wings, they hurtled out, flew across the fighting, and landed on the other side of the street.

Before Ines could say a word, Rumiel flew back, reappearing a moment later with Toby under one arm and Damon under the other. Damon was pale as a ghost, his left hand clenched tight in the right. Rumiel set both boys down beside Ines.

"This is not..." Rumiel's face was distorted by the emotions at war across it. "This does not mean..." He flapped his wings. "I must go after her."

Fire blazed as he drew his sword and headed back into the fight.

CHAPTER 21
The Battle for Manchester

"Which way to the station?" Ines asked.

They were striding away from the Museum of Science and Industry, the sounds of magical combat receding behind them.

"This way, I think." Toby pointed ahead.

"You think?" Ines looked around, trying to get her bearings. "How sure are you? Because we've got maybe half an hour to get there, and then Dad—"

"I know," Toby snapped. "I'm not just a kid. And it's this way."

But he was a kid, looking red faced and disheveled, weighed down by exhaustion. Ines might not be able to look after him, but she still needed to find someone who could.

Someone like Dad.

Toby broke into a run, and she followed, careful to keep Damon in sight as he ran beside her. Neither of her boys was fit enough to run far, and she didn't want to leave them behind.

Dusk was closing in, streetlights flickering on as the sky turned a darker shade of gray. A light spattering of rain fell on them, dappling the street and sticking loose strands of hair to Ines's forehead.

The flames of a burning car lit the way ahead of them, raindrops hissing as they evaporated in its heat, greasy smoke swirling away. Similar black pillars rose above the rooftops from nearby streets, twisting in the wind, streaking the sky with the ghosts of destruction. Half the shop fronts they passed had been broken open, shutters buckled and windows smashed. The rear end of a BMW lay across the pavement, its front inside an electronics store. Half a dozen televisions lay broken amid the shards of window glass.

There were bullet holes too. More than Ines had ever seen outside a movie. More than she wanted to think about. There was no way bullet holes could be a good sign, especially when some of them were accompanied by bloodstains.

"Lancasters," a voice bellowed from up ahead. "Attention!"

The words were followed by the sound of hundreds of feet all slamming into place at once.

The three of them stopped running, pausing to peer around a corner, into a park to their left. A soldier stared back at them from a dozen yards away. He wore a uniform in camouflage grays, helmet strapped into place, his gun pointing to the ground at their feet. He showed no surprise at their appearance but kept his eyes fixed on them.

Behind him stood more soldiers, all with their backs turned to Ines. It was hard to tell, but she thought there were at least two hundred of them, stood stiffly at attention. Facing them was another man in uniform, his hair dappled the same grays as his uniform, looking over his troops from a vantage point of standing on a bench.

A demon hung in the air above him, rubbing its claws together as it watched the gathered troops.

"You've all seen what's out there," the commander roared. "The menace plaguing our streets. Abominations from who knows where. Armed gangs destroying the rule of law. Shady agents of a so-called government Ministry trying to usurp authority. Blood and revolution staining the streets of our country. We're here to stop that.

"We've lost people already. Good men and women cut down in their prime, first by those thugs from Sale, then by the traitors in the Greater Manchester Police. Those bastards have taken our friends. They and the people they answer to want to take our country. Will you stand for that?"

"Sir, no, sir!" the entire assembly bellowed.

"Then will you stand with me?"

"Sir, yes, sir!"

"Will you stand for order?"

"Sir, yes, sir!"

"Will you stand for security?"

"Sir, yes, sir!"

"Will you stand for this once green and pleasant land?"

"Sir, yes, sir!"

The demon expanded with each shout, its belly bloating, spines spreading from its head. Its mouth opened wide, revealing rows of glittering teeth. None of the soldiers even saw that it was there.

"We should go," Damon whispered. "Before they start on whatever they're going to do."

"And before Dad's gone," Ines said.

She looked again at the guard facing them. He still showed no signs of movement.

"Come on." She ran past the park, the others following her, and on up the road. Behind them, the commander had started giving out orders to his troops.

An old building in pale brick and orange stone rose to the left, its ground floor boarded up, weeds hanging from gutters and window ledges. Beyond it was a junction.

"The back way in is up there." Toby pointed. "I was looking on maps earlier."

Gunfire erupted, the sound echoing from the tall buildings. A streetlight at the junction shattered. Seconds later, a bottle exploded against a traffic light, its contents bursting into flames.

A car skidded as it reached the junction, sliding to a halt sideways on. The driver leapt out then fell across the bonnet, blood pouring from his leg. More bullets shattered the windows as several men and women ran up and took shelter behind the car. Every few seconds, one of them would rise, fire a few shots at someone farther down the street, and then duck back into cover. The driver crawled in beside them, clutching his wound.

"Is there another way in?" Damon asked.

"Yes," Toby said. "Back where those guys came from. If we want to avoid this, then we'll have to go a long way around."

Ines glanced at her watch. Their time was almost up. Any moment now, the Ministry of Occult Affairs would be putting her dad on a train, sending him away to who knew where. They might already be too late, and they definitely would be if they didn't get into the station soon.

"There's no time," she said. "We have to find a way through this."

She wished she had a gun, or better still, her knives. She didn't have much experience with guns, but she'd been getting used to those knives. They gave her a way of dealing with problems. Though even they couldn't have protected her from a spray of bullets.

As if the universe had heard her need, the people behind the car scurried back the way they had come, firing over their shoulders as they retreated up the street. No sooner was the way clear than more armed figures came to take their place, ducking behind the other side of the car. This time they were police, some in flak jackets and carrying guns, a few with batons and riot shields. None of them looked in the mood to help young people in trouble.

Glancing at her watch, Ines once again found herself bowing to the inevitability of the least bad option. She didn't want to do it—the potential cost was huge—but she couldn't see another way.

"Use your power," she said to Damon. "All your power. Whatever it takes to get us through."

"You're happy for me to do that?" he asked.

"Happy? No." Ines shook her head. "Desperate? Yes."

His expression was torn, his mouth splitting in a grin, his eyes as full of fear as they were of creeping black veins.

"Alright, then." He stepped out into the middle of the street. In one hand, he clutched his pocket watch. The other was raised before him, a black spot on the back matching the one Ines had seen on the palm. The air rippled around him as he started to chant in a deep, menacing tone.

Damon's hand pulsed, darkness swirling out of it. Black tendrils writhed in the air. Not the time magic she had first seen him use, but the pure force of Hell. His voice rose, the chanting becoming more urgent, and the darkness spun, its ends flaying the road and surrounding buildings.

Magic poured off Damon. His pale skin was replaced by a layer of midnight black. His very presence seemed to swallow the light. The only point of brightness was the watch still clutched in his left hand.

One of the police officers saw what was happening. Turning her gun on Damon, she opened fire. Bullets gouged the street, but when they hit the demonic magic, they were swallowed whole. The officer yelled, and her colleagues turned to face Damon too, letting fire with their guns.

But it wasn't the bullets that made Ines afraid. It was that blackness, wild and unstoppable, threatening to swallow her friend forever. He wasn't even directing it. The power was consuming him.

The gangsters reappeared, rushing the police while they were distracted. The junction erupted into a massive brawl as the two sides attacked each other with everything from pistols to cricket bats.

Then Damon raised his left hand. His voice changed, no longer the tone of a demon, but that of the young man she knew. The blackness surged off of his body, revealing the human underneath. It coalesced in a dark orb in front of him. He reached out with his watch. It seemed to soak up the power as it touched it, the orb shrinking away until there was nothing left. Nothing but a shimmering in the air around Damon, a haze in which bullets stopped, hanging frozen in time.

He grinned and raised both his hands.

"What's the time, Mr. Wolf?" he asked. "No time at all."

The fighters at the junction froze. Police and criminals alike stood unmoving. Even the flames emerging from the car's engine stood still.

With a sparkle in his eye, Damon turned to Ines.

"I don't mean to brag," he said, "but did you see that?"

"Can we get through it?" Ines asked.

"Oh yes."

"And is time frozen in the station too?"

"No." He shook his head. "Only here."

"Then we have to hurry." She smiled back at him. "That was amazing, but we have a train to catch."

CHAPTER 22
Dad

They ran through the smashed remains of glass doors, up a series of unmoving escalators, and into the main hall of Manchester Piccadilly station. An eerie quiet surrounded them—no bustling people, no announcements of arrivals and departures, no sound of trains coming in and out. It was made all the more unsettling by the bright artificial light, which illuminated every broken and neglected detail.

"It's like something out of a postapocalyptic movie," Damon said as they looked around the emptiness. The now familiar litter of broken glass and dropped loot was scattered in front of big-brand shops along the concourse. "Everyone's given up on normal life and gone off to join a biker gang or a zombie horde."

"Except that this isn't a film," Ines said. "It's a real apocalypse."

"I thought we were going to stop it," Toby said in alarm.

"I think it might be too late for that," Ines said.

"It's never too late." Damon turned the watch between his fingers. "There are always ways to make things better, if you have the will."

"I never thought I'd hear you being so positive about humanity." Despite their surroundings, Ines smiled.

"Not humanity." Damon winked. "Just us. Now let's go rescue your dad."

There were trains at most of the platforms. Only one was lit up inside, at the far end of the station. As they walked towards it, Ines heard the hum of its engine starting up.

"Quick!" She sprinted ahead of the others, down the line of trains and around onto the platform.

To her left was a red brick wall that rose all the way to the vaulted ceiling above the tracks. To her other side sat the train, most of its doors closed. It had sleek, modern carriages like the ones that had brought them from London, though there was a bullet hole through one of the windows.

Between the train and the wall, on a platform no wider than Ines's bedroom, stood the mages.

Oldfield was in the center. One arm hung limp at her side, and there were burnt spots on her pinstripe suit. Despite it all, she looked sleek and powerful, her expression determined.

Around her were at least a dozen mages. Some had blood on their suits, and most were missing their dark glasses. Shaw was among them, her short blond hair no longer a neat bob but instead a mess that jutted in every direction.

Ines's gaze was drawn past them all, to the figure standing beside Oldfield.

"Dad!" she cried out, unable to stop herself.

David Salgado turned to look at his daughter. He looked as scruffy and battered as the mages, not due to a hard day's fighting, but just because that was how he always dressed. His jeans were faded and paint stained, his jacket pockets sagging shapelessly from years of being filled with tools and tat. Beneath it, his woollen jumper was unraveling at the waist.

He raised his hands, which were bound together with a cable tie, and waved at Ines.

"Hello, love." He smiled. Two of his teeth were missing. As Ines looked more closely, she realized that the darkness around one eye wasn't a shadow from his floppy hair, but a black eye.

Fury burned inside her. These monsters, these so-called protectors of humanity, had hurt her father.

Damon and Toby arrived behind her, panting for breath. Her brother tried to run straight past toward their father. Alarmed, Ines grabbed hold of him and dragged him back.

"Wait," she said then raised her voice to call out to Oldfield. "Let him go."

"Why would I do that?" Oldfield sneered.

"Because if you don't, then we'll take him from you."

"Three children against a dozen of the Ministry's finest?" Oldfield shook her head. "I don't think so."

"You don't look so fine anymore," Ines said. "Half of you are barely standing."

"You don't look menacing yourselves."

"Try us." Damon tossed a coin into the air then pointed at it. The air shimmered, and the coin hung still above their heads.

"Cheap tricks," Oldfield said. "But just in case..."

Raising her uninjured arm, she turned her hand into a menacing lion's paw and pressed the claws against Ines's father's throat. His eyes widened, but as he tried to step back, another mage seized his shoulders, holding him in place.

"Surrender, or he dies," Oldfield said. "He's not the one we need anyway."

"Please, Elizabeth," Dad said. "We're friends."

"We were," Oldfield said. "Until you turned against me." She glared at Ines. "What will it be?"

Ines clenched her fists. Every instinct was urging her to fight. To tear into Elizabeth Oldfield with fists and feet. To smash her elegant features into a bloody pulp, reflecting every hurt she'd done back on her ten times over. That was what Elizabeth Oldfield deserved.

Exhausted and injured as she was, with muscles aching and blood drying on her cheek, Ines could feel the desire for action all through her body. Fighting had become like a drug, something she yearned for. It had become her first and last response at the sight of a threat.

A part of her recognised the horror of what she had done to people in those fights. She remembered a mage lying on the museum floor, a knife buried in his leg, and her stomach turned. But still the longing for violence was there, and no one deserved pain more than Elizabeth Oldfield.

She shifted her legs, ready to spring forward.

"Ines." Toby grabbed her arm. He sounded small and lost. "Please, it's Dad."

Reluctantly, she took a step back and forced her fists to unclench. With every ounce of willpower she still had, she pressed the anger down inside her.

Shaw was looking straight at her. There was pity in the mage's face.

"Is this the important work you were talking about?" Ines said, holding Shaw's gaze. "Kidnapping. Extortion. Threatening to murder a man in front of his children."

"Would you prefer it if we left the demons and angels to take over?" Shaw's voice sounded different from normal. Was she just tired, Ines wondered, or was there doubt in there? Was she getting through to her?

"Enough," Oldfield said. "Surrender, or face the consequences."

"Please," Ines said. She looked from Shaw to Toby, tears in his eyes at the thought of losing their father, and then back again.

"Very well." Oldfield flexed her claws, ready to strike. "Let's end this."

"No." Shaw turned to face Oldfield.

"What?" Oldfield said.

"This isn't what I signed up for," Shaw said. "I doubt I'm alone."

The rest of the mages exchanged wary glances as they raised their hands, ready for magic.

Oldfield started to draw her claws across Dad's throat. Shaw yelled something incomprehensible and jerked her hand up. As she hit Oldfield's arm, the magical paw burst apart, become a glowing cloud around the mages' heads.

"Stop her!" both women yelled at once.

The platform descended into chaos, gray-clad mages falling upon each other. The station was filled with the light of a dozen combat spells and the crackle of clashing magic. The minister's claws were back, darting around in the midst of the melee, and blood flew from their tips.

"Dad!" Ines rushed forward.

Damon was beside her, raising his hands to cast a spell. The air shimmered as it had in the street. Two of the mages turned toward him, and as they twisted their hands, his power faded from the air. He pushed back, the air between them glowing as their spells met. The three of them stood facing each other, hands twisting, incantations spilling from their mouths in a battle of magical wills.

Blood was running across the platform from the middle of the brawl. Ines didn't try to join the fighting. Instead, she plunged through, shoving combatants aside as she made for where Dad had been.

He lay unmoving on the cold concrete, his face pale, blood pouring from his neck.

"Dad?" Ines crouched beside him. He was so still and pale. There was so much blood. Tears ran down her cheeks, and she tried to staunch the flow.

"Dad?" she said. "Please, Dad, don't be dead. Please."

His eyelids fluttered. He let out a watery cough and looked up at her.

"Press something on the wound," he said. "I took a first aid course. They talked about pressing on the wound."

Ines could have sobbed with relief. Keeping one hand pressed against his neck, she dragged her hoodie up over her head and slid it down her arm until the thick material was pressing against his wound. She bundled it up, tying the sleeves around his neck as tightly as she dared.

Pushing himself up on his elbows, Dad looked around.

"I got to drive a steam train once," he said. "Maybe I can—"

A mage staggered past, waving at the blue cloud hanging around his head. Treading blindly, he hit Dad's leg hard, and there was a horrible snap.

Dad yelled in pain.

"I have to get you out of here." Ines pulled his arm around her shoulders and dragged him upright, letting him lean heavily on her. "Keep your weight off that leg. I'll look at it as soon as I can."

He gritted his teeth and clung tightly to her.

The fight was still going on, but somebody was winning. One group was backing away down the platform, the other following them, though more slowly, making sure they didn't regroup rather than trying to overwhelm them. With both groups made up of gray-suited mages, it took a moment to work out which side was which. Then Ines spotted Damon, glittering arcs of power spiralling around his hands. Alongside him was Tamsin Shaw, holding up a magical shield to protect them both. They had their backs to her. They were on the winning side.

At last, the retreating mages broke and ran. There was a glimpse of pinstripes in among the gray as Elizabeth Oldfield and her minions fled across the concourse, past the shattered shop fronts, and out into the night.

Toby ran up and flung his arms around Dad and Ines. For a long moment, they clung silently to each other, relishing the joy of reunion.

"Sorry." Dad's voice was ragged with pain. "Need to sit down."

With his children holding him up on either side, he hopped to a bench at the end of the platform. He stretched his broken leg out in front of him, wincing as he did it. The improvised bandage around his neck was sodden red, but the blood was no longer running freely.

"I've sent someone to search for a first aid kit." Shaw approached the bench, half a broom handle in her hand. Her right cheek was a blackened mess, the skin blistered and cracked. "This was by the doors—it should do for a temporary splint."

Damon and a mage stood nearby, watching the station in case the enemy returned. Another mage was by the doors, watching the street.

"Thank you," Ines said. "You saved us."

"Somebody had to." Shaw knelt on the ground next to Dad. Pulling a penknife from her pocket, she ripped open one side of his trousers to examine the twisted leg underneath. "I'm more worried about saving the Ministry. You were right—the minister was leading us down a dark path. We have all the most powerful mages in Britain. We need to make our choices more carefully."

"Will your colleagues back you?" Ines asked.

"Some of them," Shaw said. "As you saw, there are plenty who will back Oldfield. Things are going to get very ugly, and I don't honestly know if we can win. But if we can distract them long enough for someone else to undo their mess, then it will be worth the cost."

With a jerk of her hands, she tied one last band of cloth around Dad's leg, fastening the broom-handle splint in place.

"That's what we're going to do," Ines said with determination. "Now Dad's with us, he can tell us how to fix the Barrier."

"I'm afraid not." Dad shook his head. "I've never been able to wrap my head around that business. Your mother is the one the Ministry wanted—I was just collateral, a hostage against her good behavior."

Ines slumped. She had been so desperate to save Dad for her own sake, she hadn't realized how much else she had been depending on him for.

"That said..." He picked up Shaw's penknife from the bench beside him. Opening his jacket, he slid the blade into the lining. There was a brief sound of ripping, then he set aside the knife and reached into the new hole. "Your mother's research." He held out a slim memory stick. "This is where we'll find the answers."

CHAPTER 23
TMI

There was a mezzanine floor above the station. One side was occupied by a sushi bar, its counter closed and shuttered up. On the other side was a coffee outlet, just as deserted. Between them was a row of tables and chairs. That was where the weary group settled down to rest.

One of the mages cast a spell to open up the coffee counter then went inside and turned on the machines. A few minutes later, there were plastic-wrapped muffins and cookies on the tables, and hissing sounds announced that hot drinks were on their way.

"I don't normally expect breaking and entering from government employees," Dad said. "But I won't complain."

He shifted his leg, trying to steady it on the chair in front of him, and winced as he did so. Color was already returning to his face, but he seemed tired, neither his voice nor his actions filled with the enthusiasm Ines longed to see again.

It was comforting to sit beside him, her head on his shoulder, with Toby on his other side. Not the whole family reunited, but closer than they had been for weeks. It felt as if things were starting to return to normal.

Except for Damon. He stood by the coffee counter, breaking wooden stirrers up into tiny pieces. The whole time, he never looked her way, and she was almost relieved. By the end of the fight, his eyes had been completely black, as if the pupils had expanded to occupy the orbs. Though that had receded, thick black veins remained, matching those on his hands. It made him unsettling to look at—all the more unsettling when their eyes met.

Even without catching his gaze, she could see that gloom had descended upon him. He didn't share the relief that she and her family felt, or even the nervous tension still holding up the mages. Just a lethargy that showed in his slumped shoulders and lowered head.

"Go and talk to him," Dad said, nudging Ines in the ribs. "You know you want to."

"I can't," Ines said. "I don't think he wants to talk to me. We fell out earlier."

"That's what boyfriends and girlfriends do." Dad smiled. "They fall out, then they kiss and make up."

"Dad!" Ines looked at him in shock. This wasn't the sort of thing she ever talked about with her parents. She could feel her cheeks reddening. "He isn't my boyfriend."

"He totally is," Toby interjected. "I've seen them making out and everything."

"Shut up." Ines reached around her father to punch Toby in the arm.

"It's okay, Ines," Dad said. "I was young once too, snogging your mother in public, finding hidden places to—"

"Dad!" both siblings said at once.

"TMI," Toby said then, seeing the confused look on their father's face, explained, "Too much information."

"Huh." Dad tilted his head to one side. "I like that one. Might have to save it for when people talk too much in meetings."

"That's not really how it works," Ines said.

"And this isn't how relationships work," Dad said. "Not the ones worth pursuing. That boy clearly loves you, and given how much time you used to spend together I assume you're just as daft about him. So go talk, sort it out. Or do you want me to still be saying this to you when we find your mother?"

Having Dad talk to her in this way was bad enough. The idea of trying to have a conversation with Mum about romance was far too much. Ines sat up, mustering her thoughts.

What could she say? Damon had made his feelings pretty clear earlier. He didn't want to be involved with her, and she understood that. She'd had him following her around while she fell for Rumiel. If he'd liked her back then, it must have been horrible for him. Could she really ask him to forget all that, to accept that it was him she wanted now?

But Rumiel wasn't here—he never would be. The boy who had seemed like her guardian angel had turned out to be one more monster in a world full of them. Unlike him, Damon had stuck with her through all of this. They had so much in common, enjoyed each other's company so much. He was her best friend, the rock that had held her up through this crisis.

The more she thought about it, the more she realized that those thoughts were what she needed to say, not just to herself, but out loud to Damon.

She looked up at him. He was looking at her, but he turned away as soon as their eyes met. The mage behind the counter put a cup of coffee down next to Damon, who grabbed it and stalked off around the corner of the mezzanine.

Ines's heart sank. Was it really that bad, that he didn't even want to look at her?

"Go after him." Dad spoke more quietly this time. "You'll have some privacy now."

He winked, and Toby rolled his eyes.

"Okay." She stood, made her way out through the awkward gap between tables, and followed Damon around the corner, her heart racing as she went.

There was another seating area this side of the mezzanine, space for customers who'd chosen the fried-chicken place for lunch. The tables were overturned, metal chairs in jumbled heaps. Damon leaned on the barrier by the mezzanine's edge, looking out at the concourse below.

Walking quietly, as if she were approaching a nervous pet, Ines went to stand beside him.

"It's not much of a view," she said and immediately felt like an idiot. Of course it wasn't much of a view. It was some escalators, another coffee stand, and a bunch of platforms. What did you expect in a station?

"I don't know," Damon said. "There's something admirable about the ability to make something so utterly bland. Like they really put the effort into taking all the charm out of this place."

Ines smiled. This was the Damon she'd missed in the last few hours—the sly sense of humor, taking pleasure in humanity's absurdities.

That thought caused another double take. Had only a few hours of his bad temper made her miss the sweeter Damon? Maybe Dad was right.

She leaned on the barrier next to him, and their arms touched. For a moment, she felt a tingle of excitement at the contact. Then he stood upright, breaking the connection, took a sip of his coffee, and stared at her.

"What do you want, Ines?" he asked.

The ice in his tone froze her in place.

"I just wanted to talk." Her heart was racing again, but not with excitement as it had before. Tension filled her. Dread even, absurd as it seemed to worry about this after everything they'd been through.

"Then talk." He drank some more of his coffee.

"What you said before," Ines said. "About not wanting to be with me. You didn't mean that, did you?"

He hesitated for a moment.

"I meant it," he said at last. "Otherwise, why would I say it?"

"Because of the demonic influence," Ines said. "All that dark power running through you. Taking you over. You weren't acting like the real you."

"Have you considered that this might be the real me?" As he spoke, the blackness filled his eyes once more. "After all, I am half demon."

"You were half demon before. That didn't stop you feeling the way you did then."

"Then I was rejecting my demonic heritage. Now I've embraced it."

Pulling the watch from his pocket, he held it out in front of her. Guttural sounds dripped from his lips, words that meant nothing to Ines, and a sphere of black power appeared around the watch. The darkness faded, leaving behind a shimmering in the air.

"I am not what I once was," Damon said.

Holding his cup above the watch, he tipped it over until the coffee came pouring out. As it hit the magic, it froze in place, still falling and yet going nowhere, like a photograph in three dimensions.

"I can change the power I have been given." He brought his cup around beneath the coffee and uttered another incantation. The liquid fell, splashing into the cup. "Use it for magic that is truly my own. But it is changing me too. I am not the boy you knew, and I am not done becoming what I will be."

"I don't care," Ines said. "I mean, I do care. I care about you. Whether you're a human or a demon. Whether you're wielding time magic or dark magic or no magic at all. Whether you want to be with me or not, I'll still care about you. So stop wasting my time, stop showing off, stop avoiding the subject, and tell me what you actually think, you colossal arse."

She put her hands over her mouth, shocked at the words that had come out. She hadn't realized how mad he'd been making her, not until it all tumbled out.

Caught in the horrible realization that she had probably offended him forever, she waited for his response, for the anger she deserved.

Damon laughed.

"Don't hold back, will you?" He threw the cup away, coffee spilling across the ground a dozen feet below. "Fine. No more distractions. No more excuses. No more bullshit."

The black receded from his eyes, and he looked normal again.

Not just normal. Wonderful. Proud and handsome in a way that she had never appreciated before. Confidence poured from him, and there was something marvelous in his smile.

"I love you, Ines," he said. "I've loved you as long as I've known you, and none of what we've been through could ever change that. So yes, I want us to be together. Do you?"

She grabbed him by the collar, pulling his face down to hers, and kissed him hard. They wrapped their arms around each other, and she knew what it was to be wanted—without doubt, without questions, with a certainty that made his embrace more powerful than any magic in the whole of Heaven and Hell.

For a long time, they stayed like that, lips locked, bodies pressed tightly together, holding each other so tightly, she thought they might crush themselves into a single person.

At last, she let him go, reluctantly, out of a need to catch her breath. He grinned at her, red faced and exultant.

"I'm glad your dad wasn't here to see that," he said.

"Oh God." Ines shook her head. "The worst thing is, he'd be cheering us on. He's the one who gave me the courage to come around and talk to you."

"Then I guess I should say thank you." Damon took her hand. "And we should all talk about what we do next."

The excitement rushed out of Ines like air escaping from a burst balloon. Talking about their next steps meant thinking about all the awful things that had happened up until now.

But it also meant talking about the successes they had achieved, beating Oldfield here in the station. And it meant planning to set the world to rights.

She smiled.

"All right, then." She squeezed Damon's hand and dragged him toward the other side of the mezzanine.

A sound made her stop and look across the station, through the glass wall that separated the concourse from the platforms, down the tracks and out into the world. The sound grew from a distant murmur into the beating of dozens of wings, all more powerful than any bird.

Bright with the light of holy power, the Blazing Host of Michael's angels soared towards them.

CHAPTER 24
Blood and Glass

"Angels!" Ines ran around the corner, into the area where the others had been relaxing. "The angels are coming! We have to move."

Everyone leapt to their feet, except for Dad, who dragged himself upright with a grimace of pain. At a nod from Shaw, one of the mages went to Dad's side, helping Toby to support him.

"We can fight them." Shaw spread her hands, and a net of glowing light appeared between them. "That's what the Ministry is for."

"There are more of them than us," Ines said. "We're tired and injured. I don't think we can take them."

"Very well." Shaw turned to her other mages. There were six of them altogether, including Shaw and the one holding Dad up. "Murphy, Grant, you're best at close combat—hold up the rear. Simms, get those etheric feelers out and find a path to safety. Lloyd, you're with me. Damon too."

With an almighty crash, the partitions between the concourse and the platforms gave way. Enough glass to cover a football pitch hurtled through the air, shards sparkling, shattering, tinkling as they fell.

Everyone ducked, covering their faces to avoid being hit in the eyes. There was a grunt, and when Ines looked up, Lloyd was clutching his arm, blood running from the gleaming shard that protruded through his jacket.

"This way." The mage called Simms ran between the tables, her dark hair flying, eyes glowing with power. As she reached the top of the stairs, she stopped, looking down. The glow faded from her eyes as she extended a magical club from her hand. "Too late."

The flapping of wings was all around them. Angels hovered about the mezzanine, white figures in clothes that came from a dozen different eras yet would have fitted in in none, so bright was their whiteness. Their weapons burned with a fire that hurt to look at—swords, sticks, and knuckle-dusters all blazing with the same brilliant flame. There was Sanctus, fists raised and a look of terrible fury on his face. Rumiel, his gaze almost soft, something strangely tender in his eyes. And at the head of them, Michael, his armor gleaming, the mightiest of all the host.

"Do you think I do not know what you are planning?" His voice was like the roar of a hurricane. "Did you think that I would forget you in all that has happened?"

He flapped his wings, rising until he hung in the air directly above them. Ines craned her neck to look up at him.

"All of you have sinned," Michael said. "All of you have been found wanting. You most of all, Ines Salgado, with your schemes to restore the Barrier of Mercy, to prevent the great work upon which we are entered. And you, David Salgado, so-called scholar, dabbler in ways of magic that were never meant to be. You think I do not see what is in all of your hearts? You believe that you can escape punishment?

"Bow down now, and accept your fates. We will be swift and merciful."

"I've got a better plan." Ines rolled back her shoulders, shifting into a combat stance. "You all think you're so wonderful? Go screw each other, leave the rest of us in peace."

Michael shook his head.

"Sin upon sin," he said. He almost seemed to smile. "Let judgement commence."

The wing beats grew louder as the host swept in. Around Ines, the air was filled with the light of magic coming into the world, and then the crackle of power as the weapons of mages and angels met.

An angel in a Victorian dress flew straight at her, a sabre outstretched, her mouth wide as she sang a hymn of blood and vengeance. Ines grabbed the edge of a table and heaved with all her strength. The table top swung into the angel's path at the last moment. The sword burned a hole through one side, but the angel could not stop her momentum and slammed into the wood.

Dropping the table, Ines looked around for anything else she could use as a weapon. Seeing nothing, she kicked the angel in the teeth, trying to keep her on the ground.

Another angel swooped in, and Ines backed away, pressing up against the coffee counter. She reached around behind her, pulled up a water jug, and slammed it into the angel's face. It was only made of plastic, but it broke as it hit, and one of the edges scratched across the angel's cheek, making him jump back.

In the fleeting second available to her, Ines looked around. They were completely trapped. All of her companions were confined in a space between the stairs, the coffee counter, and the barrier at the edge of the mezzanine. The barrier was only waist high, but beyond it was a drop of at least a dozen feet to the ground below, where more angels waited.

The space they were in was shrinking. Even with their strongest magics, the mages could not hold back the angels when numbers were against them. Shaw fought with cold determination, wielding two magical swords of her own, parrying blows aimed at her and at Dad, occasionally lunging in to send her opponents back. Damon too was holding his own, though he faced four angels all by himself. Spinning his watch like a flail, he froze each angel in turn. But by the time he hit the fourth, the first was already lurching back into motion, the time-freezing magic drained away by divine power. He was not making progress, just holding back the tide.

Another attacker lunged at Ines, and she backed toward the edge of the mezzanine. Her foot slipped, and she looked down to see Lloyd lying dead, blood coating the ground.

"We have to find a way out," she shouted.

"The train." Dad was leaning against a table. As he waved his hands, jets of boiling steam burst from behind the coffee counter, blasting the nearest angel. The till burst open, its drawer bouncing off the cappuccino machine and hitting the angel in the head.

"How will that help?" Ines asked. "We can't drive it. You nearly drove a steam train once—that's not the same."

"I have a way with machines," he said as a light fitting swung down, knocking the angel back.

"But how will we get there?" Ines ducked, swept the legs out from underneath an angel, and then leapt onto a table to avoid a swinging sword.

"Like this." Damon stood on the barrier at the edge of the mezzanine. He held his watch out, the glass facing open, and wound the hands backwards with his finger.

A strip of air below the mezzanine shivered. For a moment, Ines saw scaffolding, then girders, then rubble before scaffolding again. The air became empty for a second before a grass slope rose in place of the tiled floor, a narrow strip of dirt leading from the mezzanine down to the platforms.

"This place wasn't always a station," Damon said. Blackness filled his eyes, and he grinned. "And the past isn't always so distant, if you know how to reach it. Now run!"

Ines vaulted the railing and led the charge down the slope. Sanctus darted in front of her, grinning fiercely, but she didn't stop. Springing from both legs, she turned her momentum into a flying leap, slamming her shoulder into the angel's chest. They tumbled together down the rest of the slope, kicking and punching, blows from his knuckle-dusters making pain flare in her arms and face.

She wasn't going to let him stop her, not when they were so close. Reaching the bottom of the slope, she grabbed his head and slammed it repeatedly into the glass-scattered floor. Light poured like blood from the wound in his side she had inflicted in their last fight.

Sanctus twisted beneath her, and Ines felt a stabbing pain in her side. Blood flowed from around the shard of glass that Sanctus had plunged into her.

"Prepare for judgement," he grunted.

"Not today," Ines said through gritted teeth. "Not from you."

With both hands, she wrenched his head up and slammed it back down. Tiles shattered beneath him, and he went limp.

Was it better to take the glass out, or to leave it in and avoid releasing a flow of blood? Ines didn't know. Maybe Dad knew, with his first aid course.

She laughed. Dad and all his dabbling.

Her hands trembled. She felt weak and dizzy. Someone had her arm, and she let herself be dragged towards the train. But then they stopped at the end of the platform.

Michael stood before them. His whole body blazed with flames, an embodiment of divine fury. Rumiel stood behind him, sword raised. She couldn't read his expression. Everything was too blurry.

"You seek to escape me?" Michael laughed. The sound had none of the majesty with which he normally spoke. It was a cruel sound, the laugh of a man who enjoyed inflicting misery. "There can be no escape from divine justice."

"Please." Ines looked past Michael, trying to focus on Rumiel. "Please."

Both angels raised their swords.

Rumiel's sword fell, and Michael screamed with pain.

"What are you doing?" he screamed at Rumiel.

"We are meant to protect," Rumiel said. "Have you forgotten that, brother?"

"You dare to call me brother?"

Michael swung his sword, bringing it over the top of his head in a two-handed blow. Rumiel raised his blade to parry.

"Eyes!" somebody yelled, but Ines was too dizzy to make sense of the word.

The blades clashed. Bright white light filled the station.

Ines blinked. She couldn't see anything, just a gray fuzz and the black afterimage of those two blades.

"Quick." The voice was Damon's, the arm around her his. Ines staggered blindly where he led her. She had never felt so powerless, unable to see, let alone act.

All around her was the crackle of magic, the flapping of wings, the sound of running.

"They got Grant," someone shouted.

Ines stumbled up a step. Something mechanical hissed, and Damon eased her into a padded seat.

It was quieter here, the sounds of battle muffled.

"Don't move," Damon said.

"But..." She reached out towards his voice, desperate for someone to tell her what was happening.

He was gone.

Bing-bong. The noise came from somewhere near her head. It was followed by Dad's familiar tone. "This is your driver speaking. This is the any-minute-now service to wherever-we're-going. We will be stopping at—ouch—at wherever we have to, I suppose."

There was a hiss and thud of closing doors, and the rumble of an engine emerged from the other noises. The seat shook beneath Ines as the train started to move, gaining speed as it roared out of the station.

"Are we safe?" she called out, but there was no one to answer. "Please, are we safe?"

A crash filled the carriage. The noise of the train grew louder, and a cold wind whipped her face. As her vision started to return, she saw someone walking towards her. Someone white with wings.

Summoning the very last of her energy, Ines forced herself to her feet. The world spun around her as she laid her hand on the end of the glass still sticking from her side, ready to draw that awful blade and go down fighting.

"Ines." The voice was warm.

"Rumiel?" she asked in amazement. "Is that you?"

"Ines," he croaked, sinking to his knees. "Is this what it feels like to die?"

CHAPTER 25
Civil Wars

The glow of Rumiel's presence drove the fog of blindness from Ines. As she reached out towards him, her vision became clearer, and with it her view of him. Maybe it was divine magic, or perhaps it was her imagination overreacting as blood loss overtook her brain, but his features seemed clearer and more gorgeous than ever before.

Everything she had ever felt for him came back in a rush of memories.

"Are we safe?" Ines asked. She knelt in front of him, the two of them facing each other in the train carriage. Wind whipped in through a broken window, the jagged glass stained with the same blood that now oozed slowly from Rumiel, as thick and golden as honey in the dreams of a child.

"We are safe." He reached out and took her hand. "For now. But I... I am not sure how much longer I will be with you."

"Don't say that." She gripped his fingers tightly. "You can heal other people. Surely you can heal yourself?"

"To my sorrow, that is not how it works." He looked down at the long gash across his belly. "Though I know little of how it does work—it is a long time since angel fought angel, even longer since any were slain."

"Did you kill Michael?" she asked.

Rumiel shook his head.

"I weakened him," he said. "Drove him off. But he has his host, and they will find a way to heal him. I bought you time, but he will return."

"Bought us time." She could hear desperation making her voice hoarse. Whatever he had done in the past few weeks, Rumiel had come back to save her now. She didn't want to lose him again. The thought was unbearable.

"You made me better, Ines Salgado," Rumiel said with a smile. "You made me realize the error of my ways. I thought that I could make the world right only by bending it to my will. That the only way to save humanity was to force their obedience. The way that Michael sought to.

"But then I saw your actions, and I heard your words. I realized that you and your family make the world a better place by protecting each other, by caring for each other. That cannot be forced from us, but we can choose to bring it forth from ourselves.

"I chose to make the world a better place. It is worth the pain I now suffer, and whatever follows."

His eyes drooped, and the grip of his fingers felt looser.

"What follows is you getting better." Ines leaned closer. The pain of the glass in her side grew deeper, and she felt blood run hot down her thigh. She didn't care. "Do that for me too."

"I shall do my best." He leaned forward.

Slowly, painfully, they drew together and shared a tender, lingering kiss. Ines felt as if fire were running through her. Revitalized, she tried to draw him close, but the pain returned. The world spun around her.

With a groan, Rumiel toppled to the floor. Ines slumped beside him and let her eyes close. The rocking of the train seemed to lull her into sleep.

Just before the world faded away, she heard a door hiss open.

* * *

"Hot chocolate." Toby put the cup down in front of Ines. "And one for you."

He put the other cup down in front of Rumiel, eyeing the angel warily as he did it. Behind him, the rest of the group were sorting through piles of packaged food from the cupboards of the railway station cafe, trying to work out what was still edible. In the background, bland music played on repeat over the speaker system, some kind of emergency broadcast channel still transmitting over the radio.

"You do not fear me, boy?" Rumiel asked.

Toby pulled a face.

"You healed Dad," he said. "Some of the way, at least. That makes up for some stuff."

"Thank you." Rumiel leaned forward in his seat, wincing as he did so. His belly was clearly giving him great pain, despite the work Shaw and her colleagues had done to restore him. Still, he smiled like a little kid as he tasted the hot chocolate.

"Gather around." Tamsin Shaw banged her fist on the table.

Murphy and Simms, the other survivors of the Ministry mages, pulled up chairs on either side of their leader. Damon helped Dad to the row of tables they'd pulled together for the meeting. It wasn't much of a setting for a council of war, but that was what this felt like. An ominous assembly of desperate people, searching for a way to save their world, to a soundtrack of government-sponsored elevator music.

"I've looked at Dr. Salgado's notes." Shaw tapped the laptop sitting open in front of her, one of a few devices they had retrieved from the office of the small station. "There's enough information here to tell us how to fix the Barrier of Mercy, if that's what we want to do. And given everything we've seen over the past month, I think that's the only way to go. Anyone disagree?"

Nobody stirred.

"Alright, then." Shaw looked at the laptop screen, and her usual decisive expression turned quizzical. "The notes also raise questions. About the nature of the Barrier, why it's there, how it's really meant to work. What else it could do. In different circumstances, that would be the basis for some groundbreaking discussions. But right now, I think we have to press on. The metaphysics can wait."

Heads nodded in agreement. With the first serious moments out of the way, people started opening packets of food. If the rest of them were as hungry as Ines, then they could probably eat the whole contents of the cafe between them, even the moldy cakes. But hungry as she was, other concerns pressed more heavily upon Ines's mind.

"If we know how to fix the barrier, then how do we do it?" she asked.

"We need power from all sides— demons, angels and mages. The first step is—" The music from the speakers cut out, and a loud crackling interrupted Shaw, followed by a series of beeps.

"This is the news at ten o'clock," intoned a scratchy voice.

"Shall I turn it off?" Dad asked.

Shaw shook her head. "Let's find out what we can."

"First, the headlines," the newsreader continued. "Violence is ongoing in several British cities. The government has repeated its declaration of a state of emergency and reiterated the needs for citizens to stay indoors after curfew. In Europe, violence continues along the French border. Stock markets remained closed. No further news from Washington tonight, though there have been unconfirmed reports of rioting in New York, Los Angeles, and Dallas. In Moscow—"

The speakers crackled again, and then another voice emerged.

"Citizens of Great Britain, this is Field Marshal Sir Richard Brancepeth-Holmes. I speak to you tonight on behalf of the royal family and those close to them.

"As you may have heard, the Queen is missing, not having returned from her visit to Parliament two days ago. It has become clear that the prime minister is seeking, through the state of emergency, to enforce a dictatorship upon this country. It is against such people that our monarchy and its armed forces stand. I have therefore been commanded to gather troops and to move against those mustered by Parliament outside Oxford.

"It is with a heavy heart that I say this. Those who had been elected to represent you have instead deceived you. The chaos in our streets is their doing, and only war can wrest the nation from their hands. I call upon all loyal British subjects to join us in restoring this nation to greatness.

"God save the Queen. God save us all."

The speakers went silent. Around the table, the small group looked at each other in bewilderment.

"So it's civil war?" Dad asked.

Shaw nodded. "Just when I thought we had a chance to make things better…"

"We still do." Ines stood up and gazed around the table, looking each person in turn in the eyes. She saw strength there but fear as well. She had no idea how she looked, aside from pale—the result of blood loss and the pain of a wound Rumiel could only half heal. But the looks they returned her spoke of a respect she had never seen before in the eyes of her peers, never mind adults. "The damage to the Barrier of Mercy is behind all of this. Fixing that's the way to make things better, and we're the ones who know how to do it.

"Shaw, you said that it would take demon, angel, and mage power. What else do we need?"

"Being in the right place is important," Shaw said. "A site rich with religious history and power."

"Can you suggest somewhere?" Ines asked.

"Durham," Shaw said without hesitation. "Because that's where they've taken your mother, and we might need her too."

"Durham it is. If we need demon and angel power, then we need Damon and Rumiel. It's the most important thing, so Shaw, you should be the mage. And if you think you're going to rescue Mum without me, then you don't know me at all."

"Me too!" Toby raised his hand.

"No, you have something else to do." Ines turned her most serious expression upon him. "I need you to look after Dad. He's still too weak for this, and if Oldfield finds him, then she can hold him hostage to stop us acting. You two find somewhere safe, keep your heads down, and get better. I'll call you when we need you."

"Very sensible, Ines," Dad said before Toby could interject. She could see from his mischievous smile that her father understood the other purpose at play here—keeping Toby safe. Ines was no longer under any illusions that she could do it herself but knew Dad could.

"We should come with you too," Simms said, turning her dark eyes to Shaw.

"No," she replied. "I need you two to contact others from the Ministry and rally them to our side. Oldfield won't give up her position without a fight. We need all the support we can get. Start with people you trust, muster as many as you can, and meet us in Durham."

"That's settled," Ines said before anyone could come up with other questions or challenges. "We eat, we rest, and tomorrow, we hit the road."

Damon raised his cup of coffee as if making a toast.

"At the risk of sounding melodramatic," he said, "here's to saving the world."

* * *

The sun was shining as they gathered for one last time in the station car park.

"You take care, Ines." Dad hugged her, slipping something into her pocket as he'd done when she was a kid. He winked. "A surprise for the road."

"Thanks, Dad," she said. "I'll miss you. And you, Toby."

She hugged her brother so tightly that he squirmed in protest.

"I'm sorry I couldn't keep you safer than I did," she said as they pulled apart.

"You did brilliant, Ines." Toby sniffed. "And now Dad's got it covered—you go save everyone else."

Afraid she might cry if she lingered any longer, Ines said a last goodbye and got into the front passenger seat of the car. Shaw was at the wheel—the only one of them with a driver's license. Damon and Rumiel sat in the back, the atmosphere between them tense. It was a tension Ines felt within her as well—the conflict between these two young men, and between her feelings for each of them. She felt terrible for kissing Rumiel after what had passed between her and Damon, but the thought of missing that kiss was equally terrible.

What would she do?

"Don"t look so miserable," Shaw said as she started the car. "Do you know how many people have fought off angels and demons without even using magic?"

"I'm guessing not many," Ines said.

"Try none," Shaw replied as they turned out of the car park and onto an empty road. "Do you know how many other people could even do what you've done?"

Ines shrugged. "I don't know. This is all still new to me."

"Well, I know, and the answer's none." Shaw's expression was grim as she stared at the road ahead. "Which raises another question, one we've all been ignoring while we worry about the Barrier."

"What's that?"

"How can one teenager do things no one else in the world can?"

They sat in silence, Ines not knowing what to make of the question, as mile by mile, they headed north.

ABOUT THE AUTHOR

S.A. Beck lives in sunny California. When she's not surfing, knitting or daydreaming in a hammock, she's writing novels.

www.ingramcontent.com/pod-product-compliance
Lightning Source LLC
Chambersburg PA
CBHW032150190626
46814CB00005BA/1923